JALAMANTA

RUDOLFO ANAYA

JALAMANTA

A MESSAGE FROM THE DESERT

WARNER BOOKS

A Time Warner Company

Warner Books, Inc., 1271 Avenue of the Americas, New York, NY 10020

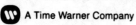 A Time Warner Company

Printed in the United States of America
First Printing: February 1996
10 9 8 7 6 5 4 3 2 1

Library of Congress Cataloging-in-Publication Data

Anaya, Rudolfo A.
    Jalamanta : a message from the desert / Rudolfo Anaya.
        p.   cm.
    ISBN 0-446-52024-1 (hardcover)
    1. Spiritual life—Fiction.   I. Title.
PS3551.N27J35   1996
813'.54—dc20   95-23716
                                                    CIP

Book design by Giorgetta Bell McRee

We will meet on the Path of the Sun,
Seeking internal clarity and peace.
We meet as brothers and sisters,
Knowing each soul reflects the other.

CONTENTS

CONTENTS

JALAMANTA

THE EXILE
RETURNS

At the end of the day, Fatimah waited by the river.

Early that morning, as was her custom, she had led her small herd of goats to the river to drink, then into the hills where the goats would graze while Fatimah watched over them. Now on her way home, she paused to look across the river.

On her side of the river, along its banks, lay the mud huts of Fatimah's neighbors, people who many years ago had revolted against the authorities and had become outcasts from their homes in the city. They then settled along the bank of the river, where they existed as best they could. Fatimah learned to survive by keeping a small herd of goats, whose milk and cheese she traded for corn and other staples.

After the revolt a wall had been built around

1

the city by the authorities. The once open and fabled Seventh City of the Fifth Sun was now at war with neighboring kingdoms.

Fatimah sighed in the gathering dusk. Thirty years ago Amado, the young man she had loved, had been exiled by the authorities of the Seventh City for daring to question their dogma. For thirty years she had watched and waited for his return. Across the River of the Golden Carp lay the southern desert, the place of Amado's exile.

Even now, Fatimah could hear his words, and the passion that rang so clear in his voice:

"The authorities use the sacred books to oppress us," he said. "The sacred books were written as signposts to guide our path. They were not written to enslave us. We must create our own path if we are to illuminate our souls."

She understood his objections, for she too believed the teachings of the moral authority had grown pedantic and restrictive. The old books of the prophets of the desert contained the knowledge needed to understand mankind's relationship to the Universal Spirit, but the interpretations of the moral authorities had grown burdensome. Those in power believed it was necessary to destroy the faith of those who hungered for a spiritual path. For the authorities, nothing could be allowed to challenge their complete control.

As a young man Amado had dared to seek a new way. He listened to the wise teachers who roamed the desert, those who from time to time appeared at the edge of the city to preach. From their insights Amado began to evolve his thoughts on caring for the soul, his way to illumination.

"The soul is an entity of light within," he said to Fatimah the day he was banished. "It is an essence that seeks clarity. But how can we achieve clarity when we are burdened with veils that hide the light? To seek clarity, one must walk the Path of the Sun. I will walk that path, and I will take your love with me."

On this afternoon Fatimah's memories were as palpable as the light of the setting sun. She felt with renewed poignancy the love they had shared so long ago.

For thirty years she kept that love alive. She had never given up hope that he would return.

Now the time of his exile was completed. The southern desert was a place of suffering, death, and forgetfulness, but Fatimah knew Amado had survived, for through the years she had heard reports from wandering tribesmen of a prophet who preached in the desert camps. They said he went from tribe to tribe, speaking of a path of illumination, and that he called himself Jalamanta, he who strips away the veils that blind the soul.

Fatimah listened eagerly to these reports. He was alive, she was sure. He had lived through his ordeal. And so each afternoon at close of day, she turned to gaze across the river. He would come, she was sure, he would come.

Even now as the sun streaked the clouds of the

3

western sky with vibrant mauve and red, she saw a figure appear in the distance. She stood and shaded her eyes. Yes, it was a man moving slowly toward the river. His long hair and beard were white, and his robe was the white cotton of desert wanderers.

She felt her heartbeat quicken.

How many times had she seen a desert wanderer cross the river and enter the city, and how many times had she been disappointed?

But her heart would not be denied. Something about the purposeful stride of the man reminded her of Amado. Could it be?

She ran to the river's edge where Clepo, the ferryman, and his dog lay sleeping by the side of the small and battered skiff.

"Clepo!" she called. "A stranger comes! Hurry!"

Clepo's mangy dog barked, awakening his master.

"What is it? What do you say?" Clepo opened his eyes and looked at Fatimah.

"A stranger approaches," Fatimah pointed.

Clepo looked. "Ay, strangers come and go. And why do they come to the Seventh City? Is it that when the end of the world is near, people gather to console each other?"

He laughed, a bitter laugh. He had ferried souls across the river for as long as he could remember. People seeking answers to the loneliness they felt within, seeking answers to the chaos and violence that surrounded them.

"Hurry, Clepo!" Fatimah commanded. "Don't make him wait!"

She could see the stranger now, nearing the opposite bank. There could be no mistake, the man was Amado! Her heart would not lie!

"Yes, yes," Clepo grumbled. He whistled for his dog, who jumped into the small boat. "I'm going, I'm going. Only for you, Fatimah, would I row across the river this late in the day."

He cast off and rowed slowly across the river, complaining. "Yes, we gather to console each other when death is near. Look around you, Tibodabi," he spoke to his dog. "Death and destruction everywhere."

It was true. Behind them the once prosperous Seventh City of the Fifth Sun was dying. The wars of the world beyond had reached this far. People without homes gathered in the streets. Children without parents wandered fearful and hungry through the rubble.

The end of the millennium was near; the end of time was near.

The man waiting for Clepo was robust and stout, but the desert's heat had withered his countenance. He held tight to his staff to steady himself.

Poor soul, Clepo thought, another desert wanderer gone in search of the Holy Grail. And what did he find? Only that the desert is cruel and full of demons.

His boat pushed against the shore.

"Old friend," the stranger greeted him. "Thank you for coming."

"Don't thank me, thank Fatimah." Clepo gestured toward her as the man climbed aboard.

He was surprised that his dog didn't bark at the stranger. Always his dog snarled in distrust at those he ferried across the river, but now he lay quietly at the stranger's feet.

"Do I know you?" Clepo asked as he rowed. He looked into the man's eyes. Yes, burning with fever, but sparkling with an inner light. The man was no ordinary desert wanderer.

"Thirty years ago you took me across the river," the man answered, his gaze fixed on Fatimah, who waited on the opposite bank.

"Ah." Clepo nodded. Now he understood Fatimah's concern. "You are Amado. Banished these thirty years by the moral authorities for heresy. Many have waited for you, including Fatimah."

"Yes, I am Amado, the same man you rowed across the river thirty years ago."

"No, not the same man," Clepo said wisely.

Jalamanta smiled. "You are right. I am no longer the youth I was. I am now Jalamanta, a man changed by time and the teachings of the desert."

"But you do not carry the staff of a prophet," Clepo said.

Jalamanta carried only the staff of a shepherd. A weathered staff made from the twisted roots of a desert tree, crowned by the carved heads of two entwined snakes. And his robe was the plain cotton attire of a desert shepherd.

"I am not a prophet," Jalamanta answered as the skiff drew near the bank.

"Ah, but many report they have heard you speak to the desert tribes. They call you a prophet."

"I am no prophet," Jalamanta said. "I only speak of the Path of the Sun. The path I have chosen to follow."

He stood as the small boat touched the bank. His legs trembled. Fatimah stepped forward and helped him from the boat. For a moment they held each other.

"Is it truly you?" she whispered.

"Yes," he replied. "The exile has returned."

She kissed his hands and touched his cheek. Softly her hands touched his lips, lips parched by the desert. She felt the fever coursing through his body.

"Fatimah," Jalamanta whispered. The woman waiting for him was Fatimah. She was there to greet him on his return. His love for her had sustained him those long years in the desert, and now the sight of her filled him with joy.

His heart rekindled with love. Love was the Holy Grail he had sought, and now he would drink from the cup.

"Welcome home," she said, smiling, her eyes full of tears.

"I am glad to be home. I have dreamed of this."

He also smiled. The fatigue of the hurried journey and the emotion of seeing Fatimah were too much to bear. He felt his legs grow weak. He stumbled, and he heard Fatimah call for help as the darkness enveloped him.

He heard voices as he collapsed, then strong arms lifted him. He was home and safe; he smiled and allowed himself to be carried.

Later, when he opened his eyes, he found himself lying on a cot, and Fatimah was pressing a cool, wet cloth to his forehead. The softness of the goat-hair mattress surprised him, as he was used to sleeping on the bare ground.

"Where am I?" he asked.

"You are home," Fatimah replied. She held a cup of water to his lips and he drank. "Santos and Iago helped bring you here."

Santos and Iago, he thought, old childhood friends. So they were still alive. He looked around. The hut was dark, except for a lantern burning over the cooking area. Pots of goat milk and fresh cheese sat on the table.

He looked at Fatimah. Her hair was gray around the temples; otherwise it was as black as the day he last saw her. The dim light reflected in her almond eyes. Her face radiated beauty as she held the cup of water to his lips.

"Drink," she said, and when his thirst was quenched, she served him a plate of goat cheese, the round flat bread of the natives, and small sweet figs from the trees in her patio.

He ate greedily, satisfying his long hunger, while admiring Fatimah's beauty in the dim light. He was ill but had forced himself to hurry to his homeland, anticipating but afraid to hope that she would still be waiting.

"What of my parents?" he asked after he had finished his repast.

"Our fathers died in the Revolution many years ago. I brought your mother and mine to live here on the bank of the river. Both died some years ago."

Jalamanta closed his eyes. He saw his parents as he remembered them from his childhood. Two energetic, lovely people, gifted musicians. They had taught him to trust himself, to guard his freedom from the manipulators of power. Now they were dead.

"I am sorry that you were alone," he whispered, and held her hands.

Fatimah sighed. "We lost everything when we were banished from the city. Here I could raise goats and plant fig trees. The authorities do not often come down to our village by the river. We are poor, but we breathe free air. The community here is friendly. Many of the elders are here. They speak to the young of the old ways. I have been content here."

He looked at her. Her complexion was robust, tanned from her days in the sun and wind. The struggle to survive had made her strong. The beauty of her youth still played in her eyes and smile.

"So there was a revolution?"

She nodded, "We took arms against the central authority. But it was too late, they had consolidated their power. Many of our fathers and brothers died, the rest were banished."

"What of Santos and Iago?" he asked.

"Iago has prospered as a wine merchant. He does business in the city. Santos spends his time reading the holy books. He is a fine scholar, but he is frail. Your return will bring new life to him. Already the people know you've returned. There is great excitement in the community."

"Excitement for an exile?"

"The people have heard that you preached in the desert. They are eager to hear your words."

Jalamanta laughed softly. That was the way it had been in the desert camps, always when he arrived in the isolated communities he was asked to speak. The armed clashes of powerful nations had reached even into the desert. Everywhere, people sensed the end of the age had come, and the violence that afflicted humanity was a warning of an impending catastrophe.

Wherever he went, people asked how the soul could be guarded in the time of chaos. Those who respected the essence within themselves sought to preserve its capacity for love. He was asked to speak of the Path of the Sun and the way to clarity.

"I didn't come to preach," he said.

"Then why?" Fatimah asked.

"Do you have to ask?" he replied. "I came for you."

"As you promised."

"I kept my promise. But I bring nothing of worldly value."

"You brought yourself," she whispered. "You are all I need." She leaned close and kissed his lips, and he felt the warm flow of her love, so familiar it seemed it was only yesterday they had last touched.

"I returned for you," he repeated.

"And I waited," she said. "But now you must rest."

He lay back down, and she pulled the wool blanket over him.

"This fine woven blanket is worthy of a king," Jalamanta said, admiring the texture and colors of the blanket. It was woven in the tradition of the old natives of the valley, those called "the ancestors" in the old legends.

"I thought of you sleeping in the bitter cold of the desert, so I wove this for you. It is my gift to you," she said.

The blanket was soft to the touch, woven with the colors of desert flowers.

"The nights on the desert are cold," he said, and thanked her for the gift. "Wrapped in this, I will sleep like a king."

"Yes, rest. You are home now," she said.

He reached and touched her cheek. "I have dreamed of you since the day I left," he whispered.

"And I have dreamed of you," she replied, feeling the warmth of love in his touch. She reached for his hands, caressing and kissing them. "It is in the power of dream that love reveals itself. You said yourself, the soul is capable of flight. I have been with you."

"And yet I bring you so little."

She placed her fingers on his lips. "Hush. Do not speak of things I do not need. You have brought joy to my soul."

He smiled. "You have not changed. You speak to me as you did when we were young. Ah, there is so much to talk about. So much to share. I do have one gift for you."

He reached into his pocket and took out a small crystal hung on a gold chain. Even in the cool shadows of her room, the crystal shimmered with green light. He placed it around her neck.

"This one thing I have kept with me. Deep in the southern desert are the pyramids of the ancestors. There on a high mountain I first spoke to the Universal Spirit, and I first saw the dance of the Lords and Ladies of the Light. The energy and love of that moment are captured in this crystal."

Fatimah touched the necklace. She looked into Jalamanta's eyes. The love they had kept alive throughout the years was vibrant between them.

"It is a beautiful gift," she said with a smile. "Now you must rest."

She placed her hand over his eyes, and in an instant he was asleep.

FATIMAH'S
LOVE

For many days Fatimah tended to Jalamanta. She fed him goat milk and cheese, watercress and wild spinach that grew along the river, figs from her arbor, blue corn mush sweetened with honey and cream, and fried hot chiles and onions rolled in the native bread.

She massaged his body and face with almond oil, and soon the parched skin grew supple and moist, and his strength returned.

During the day he rested in the shade of her arbor. From there he watched her go off with her goats early in the morning. Neighbors of the river community on their way to work passed and called a greeting but did not intrude. They knew he had crossed the desert and he had suffered, but they also knew Fatimah's reputation as a healer. In time Jalamanta would be well enough to speak.

One morning Jalamanta rose at dawn. Outside, the mother-of-pearl light suffused the valley. A soft apricot color tinted the wisps of clouds over the mountain. A glorious awakening filled Jalamanta as he watched the light fill the sky. It was at this moment, just before the Sun broke over the rim of the mountain, that he prayed.

As he stood, head bowed, the memories of people he had known and loved flooded his mind. Many masters of mind control practiced the art of arriving at nothing; he was content to let the memories be part of his meditation. He was bound to the Earth and its people, and so he was bound to the relationships that he had forged.

He thought of childhood, his parents, his grandparents, who had settled the land and built the Seventh City, and he thought of the tribes he had visited in the southern desert. Many wise men and women had helped him see the way. Fatimah appeared as a young woman, and he remembered the day he first tasted her lips. He smiled. All these memories were pleasant, for the free flow of memory was the first step of meditation.

Along the river the leaves of the giant cottonwood trees shivered in the cool of morning, like his soul shivering in the presence of the rising Sun. River willows and tamarisks swayed as the morning breeze swept through the valley.

Fatimah appeared at his side and he turned to greet her.

"Did I disturb you?" she whispered.

"The beloved never disturbs," he said, putting his arm around her shoulders. "My meditation is a thanksgiving. I was thinking of those who have helped me. Thanks to your healing powers, today I am ready to become a shepherd again," he said. He gazed into her clear, dark eyes. She had brought him back to health, and his love for her burned in his heart.

At that moment the first rays of the Sun came over the crest of the mountain, reminding him that the light within was not to be hoarded, but shared.

He leaned and touched his forehead to hers.

"I offer you the kiss of life," he said, feeling the surge of love flowing between them, the energies of their souls becoming a filament of light in the stream of sunlight.

"I have waited long for your kiss. Today my soul becomes one with yours," she answered.

For a moment they were one with each other and the beauty of the morning. Then, holding hands, they turned to watch the Sun rise. The first spears of light filled the desert and the valley, and the dance of life began.

"This is the most precious and holy time of day," Jalamanta whispered. "As we meditate on this moment, we can feel the essence of the First Creation, that moment when the darkness of the universe gave way to light. Now the Giver of Life comes to renew our vitality and energy. In the desert the old men sing chants and call him Father Sun."

"He is a kind ancestor," Fatimah said, "like the souls of those departed whisper to us, the Sun whispers: I will nourish life."

"See how the light penetrates everything," Jalamanta said. "These are the Lords and Ladies of the Light, the male and female energy of the Parent Sun speeding across dark space to dissolve the night. Everything they touch joins in a dance of life."

Together they watched the burst of sunlight glistening and dancing on the leaves of the trees. The river reflected the light and shimmered like diamonds. The stone mountain and the fleet deer, tree and stone, man and woman, the fish of the river and the sea, the birds of the air, all were filled with light, the dance of life.

Jalamanta raised his arms and said a prayer of thanksgiving. He asked the Sun to bless all of life. He turned to each of the four sacred directions, cupping the light in his hands and offering it to each direction. He gave thanks for the new day, and again cupping his hands, he poured the light over his head so it might wash through his soul. Fatimah did likewise.

When they had washed themselves in the light, they stood in silence, commingling with everything around them as the Sun cleared the mountain crest. Light and breeze shimmered and stirred in the trees and plants. Birds sang in the trees, in harmony with all the other sounds of stirring life.

Children leading small herds of cattle, sheep, and goats to the river paused to greet Jalamanta, then continued on their way.

Fatimah looked at Jalamanta. His face was radiant with morning light. He had recovered from his arduous journey, and the people were eager to hear from him.

"The Sun fills you with light and heals you," she whispered.

"Yes," he replied, taking her hands in his. "I am well now because of you."

"The light of the Sun is greater than anything I may have done," she said.

"The Sun is a reflection of a Universal Light that has filled the universe from time immemorial," he said. "Without it there would be no life. To allow its light to fill the soul is to walk on the Path of the Sun. But the soul is also nurtured by the healing touch of love. There is no greater love than that touch which nurtures and heals."

"You have found the illumination of the Universal Light," Fatimah said, "and yet you still praise the human touch."

"The body is the temple of the soul, and so the light passes from one body to another. The soul infuses the body, as everything is imbued by this light that we see descending from our Sun."

Fatimah smiled. Her heart sang with joy. Body and soul were united in love.

"Come," she said, "let us eat and prepare for the day."

"Gladly," he said as they entered her kitchen. "Today I am strong enough to go with you."

"As it was when we were young."

"Yes." He smiled, remembering the days they had spent along the river. There in that innocent time their love had grown. They had spent many hours talking about the mystery of life, the secrets of the universe.

What was the meaning of life? they had asked each other. What is the essence within that yearns to be fulfilled? How can we care for the soul and walk the right path of our ancestors? How can we achieve that clarity of consciousness that unites us with the Cosmos.

Her love stirred his blood.

Soul, body, and mind should work in harmony and not be opposed, the young Amado said.

The body responded to desire and felt pain. The body also grieved its own mortality. The mind sought knowledge to build its empire, but it too was part of the mortal body. Only the soul could transcend the limitations of mind and body. It yearned to be one with the Universal Light.

"I remember everything," she said. "Our love was of the flesh and of the soul. Our love was a bonding that brought clarity, harmony, and joy."

"Ah, there is so much to talk about," he said as they ate. "Even now as I stood meditating, the memories came to me."

"Yes," Fatimah agreed, "our separation has been long. But now there is time."

And so they worked together, and at the end of the day, they ate their supper, then sat in the arbor. As the Sun set, its light reflected on the mountain to the east. Turtle Mountain seemed to drink in the light of the setting Sun. It glowed with energy and reflected it back to the people of the valley. The Earth's soul was reflected in the caressing light.

Santos and Iago, his childhood friends, came that afternoon to visit Jalamanta.

"We are overjoyed you have recovered your health," Santos said, kissing the hands of his childhood friend. His brown eyes filled with tears. Now his hair was as gray as Jalamanta's, but his enthusiasm was that of a young man.

"I had good care," Jalamanta said, with a smiling look at Fatimah.

"Ay, she does have the magic. People come to her and she prescribes her herbs and massages away their pains. Her reputation as a healer has spread."

"Simple things my mother taught me," Fatimah replied. "People bring their cure with them. I only take them to the source of the problem, and the light does the rest."

"It's her beauty that does the trick," Iago said, glancing at Fatimah. He had grown fat and prosperous. His gown was made of fine silk, something none of the others could afford. Why he didn't move into the city no one knew; his ways were secretive.

"I agree," Jalamanta said. "The beauty of her soul is revealed. She walks the Path of the Sun."

"Ah, the old heresy," Iago said, growing irritated. "Are you still preaching those ideas that got you in trouble in the first place?"

He looked from Fatimah to Jalamanta and saw they still loved each other. The woman the three had admired and desired as young men had waited for Jalamanta.

"My desire has been to grow in clarity," Jalamanta replied. "This is what the elders of the desert taught me."

"Ay, but that kind of talk can get you into trouble with the authorities," Iago warned. "As before."

"But he is a free man," Fatimah interrupted. "He has served the years of his exile."

"Yes, but you know Iago is right," Santos said, nodding. "The central authorities will not take kindly to anyone who speaks against their doctrine. We have no freedom. Everyone is closely watched. Brothers have turned against brothers. People who never quarreled now accuse their neighbors of senseless abuses. Tribes have turned against tribes in a bloodletting that strikes fear in us all."

"Yes," Jalamanta said sadly. "This era is ending, and instead of a peaceful transition into the new millennium, violence spreads its destructive tentacles. But a new birth may come even from the chaos around us."

Iago smiled. "Even during hard times some may

profit. I sell wine from my vineyards and do very well. Those that sell goods to the military do well. I don't complain."

"Be quiet, Iago," Santos hushed him. "We are speaking of more important things than profit. Go on," he said to Jalamanta.

"As this age ends," Jalamanta said, "the negative and positive forces within each of us struggle for control. We are leaving behind us the age of the Fifth Sun, and the time of the Sixth Sun is coming into being."

"Must a new time always be born in violence?" Fatimah asked.

"The death of an era is always violent," Jalamanta replied. "The very coming into being is a violent act. The First Creation took place in chaos. The germ of creation lies in chaos."

"What will this new age be like?" Iago asked, acting interested for the moment. He wanted to please Fatimah.

"It is said by the prophets of the desert that the new era will be a time of peace and brotherhood."

"Ah, but why so much violence to get to peace?"

"The prophets say that the forces of evil will not allow the new era to come into being without a struggle. Life will not end forever, but it will be greatly changed. Chaos will reign if we allow it, or peace and order will rule. We fear the end of time because we cannot see beyond it. But out of chaos peace may be born. It is up to us to light the way, to imagine the new era. We must be creative, for the forces of violence and chaos are inherent in the universe."

"So you tell the people it is up to them," Iago said. "They can actually create the new time."

"Yes," Jalamanta replied.

Iago laughed. "All those years in the desert made you an optimist. People don't have this power you speak of, and if they did, they would only use it to help themselves. Human nature is against you, my friend."

"Human nature is what we make it," Jalamanta replied. "If we strip away the selfish veils, we can work together to create the new era."

"Even if it means trouble with the authorities?" Santos asked.

"I will speak my mind," Jalamanta answered.

And so they spoke late into the night, discussing the essence of human nature and the way to clarity and peace. It grew late, and Fatimah saw that Jalamanta grew weary. He was still not completely recovered from his journey across the desert.

She sent Santos and Iago away, explaining that Jalamanta needed rest.

They went off into the dark of night, their shadows rousing the barking of neighboring dogs, their shapes disappearing into the deep night that rested over the valley.

But Iago did not go directly home. Troubled as he was by the return of Jalamanta, he hobbled toward the center of the city and the dark citadel of the central authorities.

Thirty years ago jealousy had filled his heart as he watched the love between Fatimah and Jalamanta grow, and now envy coursed anew in his blood.

After Jalamanta was exiled, Iago had gone to Fatimah and asked her to be his wife, but she had refused him. She would wait for Jalamanta, she said. No one ever returned from an exile in the desert, he had argued, but she would not be swayed.

Now Jalamanta had returned. Weakened from the desert crossing, but with a light glowing in his eyes. The same light shone in Fatimah's eyes. Their love had not died.

Iago seethed with jealousy as he stood before the gate of the city. It was he, his demons said, who deserved the love of Fatimah. For thirty years he had watched and waited, the lust within him a raging fire.

His heart called to him one way, then the other. But nothing could dampen the flames within him.

THE YOUTH
GATHER

As Jalamanta and Fatimah walked along the river's edge, a small crowd gathered around them. The young people from the river villages gathered to hear him speak. They had heard his story from their parents, and now they called him a prophet.

Violence touched the lives of the young. The central authorities taught a militaristic dogma and pressed the young into military service. All knew the way of the authorities only created more violence. All were eager for peace.

Jalamanta and Fatimah sat beneath a giant cottonwood at the bank of the river, the same tree that thirty years ago had been a sapling. Now it shaded those who gathered to ask questions.

"What are you called?" a girl asked. "The rulers

in the city all have titles: doctor, lawyer, priest, teacher, diviner, sorcerer, or witch."

"I am a seeker," Jalamanta replied. "I have wandered in the desert seeking the truth."

The crowd nodded. The forthrightness of this man suited them.

"Do you call yourself a prophet?" a young man asked.

"The people of the southern desert called me a prophet because I took the ancient wisdom and transformed it into a language the heart can understand," Jalamanta answered. "I am that desert wanderer who has returned home to share what I learned."

He looked around him and saw the sons and daughters of his childhood friends. They had remained in the Seventh City of the Sun to raise their families and earn their living. Only he, Jalamanta, had been forced into the desert for his beliefs.

For a moment a cloud of doubt filled his soul. Could he answer the questions of the children, or had he sought answers for questions without answers? Were there ever final answers to the questions that troubled the world?

Dispel the doubt, he whispered to himself. You have crossed the desert and spoken to the elders of many tribes. They have shown you the Path of the Sun. Walk with clarity in your heart, and speak with clarity. Everything else will give way to that truth.

"Your name has a meaning," the girl said.

"When I was born, my mother called me Amado, which means beloved. She named me in the language of her tribe. In the desert I became a new person, and during my initiation my guide named me Jalamanta. *Jala* means to pull, and *mantas* means veils. I am Jalamanta, he who pulls away the veils that blind the soul."

"What do you mean by veils on the soul?" a youth asked.

"A veil is an illusion that blinds the soul," Jalamanta answered. "Anger, hate, bigotry, greed, excessive pleasures and gratification, and many other selfish desires take possession of the mind and body. When one gives in to those desires, the care of the soul is neglected and forgotten. Those veils block the clarity of vision that we seek. Those veils block the nourishment of the soul. I teach a way of knowledge, a way to remove the veils that blind the soul."

"Where do these veils come from?" the youth asked.

"The veils that blind the soul have their origin in the distrust we have for each other," Jalamanta answered. "Time matures the mind into an entity with a will. The self is created. When that self cannot reach out to others, we grow separate from each other. To create the self is natural, but we must not forget we also belong to the community of souls."

A very arrogant young man stood. "I have great

skills and talents, and I come from a special tribe. Why not use my abilities to care for myself?"

"Respect and use your talents," Jalamanta answered, "but don't let your ego separate you from others. As children our youthful souls did not repel one another. That youthful community of souls tells us that we can live in harmony and peace with each other."

"Has this age of violence come because we stand opposed to each other?" a girl asked.

"Yes," Jalamanta answered. "The mind separates itself from others, but the soul speaks the language of the universe. It is attracted to a wider community. If we look at another person only as a self, we see differences. If we look at others as possessors of a soul, we see ourselves reflected in them. The lover beholds the soul of the beloved, and so the will of self falls away. The union of souls is love."

"We see so much suffering around us. Tribes turn on tribes, nations are at war with nations. Is this the end of time on Earth?" a boy asked.

"History teaches us that the cycles of time die. A day is born and dies, the Moon completes its cycle around the Earth, years come and go. Even stars are born and die. All that we know is born and passes away. Our body and mind enter the stream of time and are made strong. But we may also be weakened by all the world has to offer. Temptations come, and body and mind eagerly acquire the materials that weigh down the soul."

"What you say is true," said a young woman who had studied religion. "We become sinful creatures."

"Only because we separate ourselves from the Universal Light," Jalamanta replied. "The era that ends need not return to chaos. We can create the new era that is dawning."

"What do we need to do?" an elder asked. He had listened thoughtfully to Jalamanta's conversation with the young.

"We must learn anew to trust the power within ourselves," Jalamanta replied. "Each one of us reflects the mystery of the universe. Each of us has a consciousness that partakes in the soul of the universe. When we understand this and see the same power in everyone, we learn to trust ourselves and others. That trust is the love we share with humanity. The poor man and the king, the poet and the materialist, all have a purpose in life. Our purpose in life is to arrive at new levels of awareness and clarity, and that clarity that we create in the soul becomes part of the consciousness of the universe."

"A noble purpose," one of the elders said. "The young should learn that life is not to serve only the mind and the body. They have been too glorified at the expense of the soul."

"That belief is a veil that must be removed, for it is the soul that is bound to the Light of the Cosmos."

"What of the central authorities?" another elder asked. He had lived long enough to be cautious. Perhaps the youth would believe this desert wanderer, but his words were heresy. The soul belonged to the moral authorities, not to the cosmos. "They exercise complete power over us. Will they allow you to preach this doctrine of trust?"

Fatimah touched his hand, and Jalamanta sensed her concern. Both knew there were some in the crowd who would report his answer to the authorities.

"I do not need permission from the authorities to preach the truth of my heart," Jalamanta answered boldly. "To keep you enslaved, the authorities teach distrust. I say that once you find clarity of soul, you will trust every other soul. It is that power to trust and not doubt that the authorities fear."

Some of the elders frowned. The thirty years of exile had not changed the beliefs of Jalamanta. As a young man he had denied the power of the authorities over his life. The years in the desert had aged him, but had they made him wiser?

Iago had been standing hidden from view behind a grove of river willows. Now he stepped forward.

"You dare to question the dogma of the authorities?" he said. "Without the laws imposed by them, we would live like animals, killing each other like beasts in the jungle."

"But we live like that already," a youth said, jumping up to face Iago. "Look at the violence and poverty of spirit around us. Perhaps the prophet is reminding us of something we have lost."

"Yes," a young woman said. "We are sick of despair. It has been so long since anyone spoke of trust and of the soul. Please, tell us more," she said to Jalamanta.

"You must learn to trust the essence within," Jalamanta replied. "The soul responds to truth and peace. It resonates to the spirit of others, as well as to the imaginative power of the universe. When you surrender yourself to those who claim to hold the only truth, you have forsaken the trust in yourself."

"You say to trust in myself means to nourish the clarity of my soul," Iago said.

"Yes."

"But doesn't that lead to the very chaos you want to control," he persisted. "Every soul will trust itself and make its own rules! Then it's every man for himself, grabbing what he can."

"Isn't that what we already see," the young woman said. "Everyone grabs what he can, and it serves only to increase the violence and mistrust."

Jalamanta looked at her and nodded. "The world is in love with the things it creates. I ask you to know the nature of your soul. You will recognize that essence in others. Trust in oneself also means to trust others. By giving your soul over to the authorities, you have become powerless, and they have become your master."

"But to say we must take away the power of the central authorities is to preach revolution!" Iago exclaimed.

"I preach a revolution of the spirit," Jalamanta said. "When we gather together to put aside our distrust in each other and to respect the essence within each person, we practice that revolution. To free the soul of its veils is to create a community of souls. There lies the true peace."

For a moment the elders in the crowd were silent. The prophet had admitted he preached revolution. He would wrestle away the power from the authorities and place it in this community of souls he talked about. As much as they yearned for the peace of which he spoke, they wondered if giving up the laws of the regime would only bring greater devastation. Perhaps they had been enslaved so long, they no longer recognized the free soul.

"I agree with you," a boastful young man said, having misinterpreted what Jalamanta said. "I call no man master! I see those who hoard gold, and so I steal from them to satisfy my needs!"

On his arms shone gold bracelets. From his ears hung gold earrings. His fancy jacket shimmered with gold threads.

"What you take weighs you down, as it once weighed down its owner," Jalamanta replied.

"What do you mean?" the young man asked.

"Look at how you guard all you carry. Now you have to sleep with one eye open to guard the gold-embroidered jacket you stole from the rich man. You put many locks on the machine you stole for transportation."

31

The crowd looked at the young man. Jalamanta was right. The more he took, the more he became like those from whom he stole.

"So you are going to tell us to put away everything we own?" the young man asked. "We have already heard the preachers tell us to put away worldly goods. And what we put away, they accumulate."

"I teach you to trust the essence within," Jalamanta answered. "Your real power comes from within, not from the gold you possess."

"So I must put aside my love of the world?" the young man said.

"No, you must love this Earth," Jalamanta replied.

Whispers of doubt filtered through the crowd. The great prophets of the past had taught that the way to heaven was to renounce the world.

"How can we love this Earth and enter heaven?" an old man asked.

Jalamanta raised his arms in praise. "The four sacred directions of the Earth reflect the four directions of the Cosmos. I say, love this desert teeming with life, this river that waters your crops and animals, these trees that provide fruit, and woods of mountain that provide fuel for your homes and fireplaces. Love the animals of the Earth, bird and beast, fish and fowl. This Earth so filled with the light of the Sun reflects the expanding Cosmos. Its beauty is a dream of splendor. The gift of light flows through everything, both the living and the not-living. The energy of the Sun permeates the Earth, and the Earth lives. Yes, you should love this Earth."

Some shook their heads, but one young woman stood and spoke: "I sometimes feel this beauty you speak of. I meditate, and my soul seems to dissolve into the beauty of the Earth. I feel connected, and time ceases to flow."

"You have described the Path of the Sun, the path of beauty." Jalamanta smiled. "Each person has the power within to join the essence of the soul to the essence of the Earth."

"Yes, the essence of the Earth," the young woman repeated. She understood his words. "Sometimes I feel I could reach out and touch the spirit of the Earth. I feel it in my entire being, then veils descend, and I am trapped in a dark labyrinth."

"The veils of life shroud the soul. You must strip away the veils to arrive at the essence of light at the Center," Jalamanta said.

"How?" she asked with anguish in her heart.

She understood his words, for she had felt the mystery of life surround her—in the trees and river, stones and mountain, sky and clouds. It was there before her eyes, and she had reached for it. She yearned to understand its message. She yearned for communion, but she had caught only brief glimpses.

"Allow the clarity of the Sun to fill your soul," Jalamanta answered.

"Tell me how?"

"Come," Jalamanta said. "Close your eyes and

turn for a moment toward the Sun. Allow the clear light to penetrate your thoughts, your body, your soul. Meditate on that light, and allow it to dissolve the veils that obstruct."

She did as he instructed. Closing her eyes, she turned toward the morning Sun and bowed. First the rays warmed her, and the sensation was pleasant. Then for the first time she felt the light entering her body, penetrating the flesh. Something within responded to the light, like a third eye opening to a wisdom just beyond the veil.

"The veils of darkness have fallen away," she said softly. "I feel a lightness."

"Clarity is lightness," Jalamanta answered, "for the universe vibrates with light. The light touches the soul, and the soul recognizes the light of the First Creation. We are the light that flows throughout the universe, we are the light that is the Universal Spirit."

The young woman opened her eyes and looked around her. In those brief moments the world had already changed. She took a deep breath and felt the energy course along her spine.

Jalamanta smiled. "You are now on the Path of the Sun."

"This is something I can do every day?"

"Yes," Jalamanta answered. "With this meditation you will learn to put away the doubts that have been instilled in you. You will begin to see which desires are false, and you will find a path of your own choosing."

"Why has it been so difficult to believe in myself?" she asked.

"The mind grows strong, creating many selves within its sphere. Each self seeks the fulfillment of its own desire. When the mind is cluttered with the demands of the selves, the conflicting desires cloud the soul, and when the mind and soul are in strife, a disharmony is created. The diverse energies of the mind become the veils to be stripped away if clarity is to fill the soul."

"That clarity of light comes through meditation," she said.

"Yes," Jalamanta answered. "These moments spent washing your soul in the morning light is the Path of the Sun."

"But the mind is very powerful," an elder reminded him.

"Yes," Jalamanta answered, "and the mind has its own beauty. But it is a beauty that must be in harmony with the soul. When the mind and soul work in harmony, they infuse each other with energy. The inner harmony, love, and light of the soul complement the mind. The mind that clouds the soul and no longer pays attention to clarity is confused."

"I will practice this meditation." The young woman smiled and thanked him. She sat at his side.

"May your soul be filled with light," Jalamanta said.

The crowd nodded their approval. This prayer

for clarity seemed simple. The path was long, but the young woman had already felt a release.

"I find clarity and peace in this," a young man challenged. He stepped forward and held up a packet of white powder. "When I use this, I feel powerful. My mind grows clear and peaceful."

"The chemicals of this world produce a false euphoria," Jalmanta said. "To be addicted to them is to give up your clarity of consciousness. Addictions are veils that must be stripped away, for they cloud the soul. The clarity that does not radiate from the pure soul is not clarity, and the insight you claim to find in your powders is an illusion."

The young man laughed. "It is all illusion," he said. "The central authorities create the illusions! The machines of war and the images they manufacture are illusions! So why not find some relief in these magic powders?"

"The pleasure they bring is momentary," Jalamanta answered. "The doubts that drove you to the addiction are still in you. You have become a slave and do not know it."

"Yes, I am a slave to my addiction," the young man admitted. "Why not?"

"I will tell you why," Jalamanta answered. "The chemicals you use for pleasure come from outside yourself. The soul resides within. In your soul you have a tremendous power available to you, and yet you seek easy solutions from outside yourself. As long as you believe your answers come from outside yourself, those who provide the illusion will rule your life."

The young man was intrigued by Jalamanta. Yes, the chemicals he relied on came from the manipulators of souls. Was there a greater power? A greater euphoria?

"What do you seek? What is the purpose of this clarity you find?" the young man asked.

"The soul's clarity brings understanding. To gaze within is to look upon the very mystery of life. When the soul is clear it can imagine its potential. Why veil it with illusions?" Jalamanta said.

"What do I care about the mystery of life," the young man retorted.

"You are part of that mystery. To feel it is to feel connected to other souls and to the Universal Spirit."

"And what will I gain?"

"You will learn to transcend your limitations. You will come to a new awareness of your purpose in life. The pleasure and pain of body and mind can be transcended. There is a universal consciousness waiting for you."

The young man hesitated. He was intrigued by the promise in the old man's words. He was tired of his addiction. But could a soul so clouded with doubts find peace in the simple words of the prophet?

"It need not be revealed all at once," Jalamanta said, and offered his hand to the young man. "The Path of the Sun begins with the first step. Just as this young woman has taken a first step. You must decide."

The young man nodded. "I thought I was in charge of my life, but now I understand I'm being manipulated and used. I want to be free of those exterior bonds."

"Then come and join us on the Path of the Sun," Jalamanta said, and took his hand.

The crowd showed their approval by clapping and reaching out to the young man in encouragement. The elders smiled. Perhaps there was a way to break the chain of dependency that had enslaved the young.

"But I know nothing of this mystery that you say will be revealed," the young man said.

"There is no mystery," Jalamanta said. "To meditate is simply to take the time to be still for a moment. This moment of silence allows you to participate in the same imagination that created the universe. The coming into being of the universe gave birth to a universal consciousness. That consciousness is a vital force that flows throughout the Cosmos. When the pure soul communes with that force, the veils are stripped away, and the energy of the universe flows through the soul. The pure soul yearns for communion with that universal consciousness, as much as it yearns for communion with other souls. That communion creates love."

The words of Jalamanta touched the crowd.

"There can be no love as long as we are separated from each other," Jalamanta continued. "You create your aloneness. As long as you do not know your soul, you will never know the joy of communion with others. You will never feel the inspiration that comes from commingling with the Universal Spirit."

"Is it possible?" the young man asked.

"All things are possible to the pure soul," Jalamanta answered, and embraced the young man.

Jalamanta looked into the eyes of the young. Did they understand the power of the essence within, or had they grown as cynical as the age? He had met many young people in his travels and he knew the worm of cynicism ate at their souls.

Everywhere, there was a conspiracy against hope. The shrouded soul lived in fear and ignorance. Those in power used fear and ignorance to turn one person or group against the other. Those who called themselves the moral authorities no longer gave hope to the individual, they only denied their self-realization. Many felt the need to understand their predicament, but the search took seekers farther away from the essence within, and they gave their minds and souls to false prophets and cults.

Many nations ate at a trough of material goods, the rest of the world starved. Those who had plenty wanted more and ignored those who did without. The young who saw the injustice and did nothing became jaded.

The powerful worked actively to destroy self-trust. The era of the Fifth Sun was ending in fear and ignorance because it served their purpose. By creating chaos, those in power tightened their grip on the masses. They taught the young to feed on cynicism.

How could he teach them that potential within? How could he explain that their souls were the stuff of the universe, the essence of the Universal Spirit?

THE FIRST
CREATION

Look." He pointed to the Sun, which was flooding the valley with its vibrant morning light.

"The Sun rises like a lantern of wisdom to dissolve the night. Like a kind of parent calling the child from a night of dreams. Rise in the morning and pray to the Parent Sun. Pray that all of life be blessed by its energy and warmth. Allow the light to enter you and dissolve the dark veils. Allow the energy and imagination of the First Creation to course through your body and burn away the veils. The clarity of light allows you to see into the unity of things."

"That is a lovely prayer," a girl said.

"The prayers of the soul are simple," Jalamanta answered. "The prayers of the soul are a communion with light. When the soul opens itself to clarity, it learns to trust itself. It reflects the beauty of the First Creation, and so it becomes an imaginative and growing entity. That illumination also leads the soul to a communion with other souls.

"I pray for the Parent Sun to bless all of life. I raise my arms in salutation, and the Sun's clarity enters and fills me with light. The cycle of life begins anew each day. I turn to the four directions and offer the sunlight I hold in my hands to the sacred Earth. Bless all of life. Through mind and flesh I feel the sunlight penetrating me, renewing me, passing through me to enter the Earth. This sunlight is a reflection of the vital energy of the universe."

"Why only a reflection?" a young man asked.

"Reflection is all we know of the First Creation," Jalamanta answered. "The light of the First Creation is boundless in its energy. It spreads throughout the universe. We see it reflected in the farthest galaxies of the universe, in the starlight whose very dust we share. The Parent Sun is closest to us, and through its light we are blessed by the Universal Spirit."

The young woman at Jalamanta's side asked, "What is that vital energy? What is the Universal Spirit?"

"Share your thoughts with us," Fatimah said. "We have lived in a world without light for so long, the young need to hear your words."

Jalamanta nodded. The beauty of her face revealed the luminous soul within. She walked on the Path of the Sun, and still she asked him to speak.

"The soul of the universe has its beginning in the First Creation. A coming into being is a coming into consciousness. That act of imagination inherent in the First Creation is also an act of Divine Love. It expands throughout the universe, and that love is what I call the Universal Spirit."

"Speak to us of that First Creation," the elders said.

"How can we speak of the formless?" Jalamanta said. "How can we speak of an energy inherent in chaos? Out of that nothingness came the boundless universe. Our words fall short when we speak of the imaginative spark of love. Our own Sun is a product of that First Creation, so I describe the First Creation as I describe each new day. The Lords and Ladies of the Light come streaming to Earth each day, and they bring life and clarity. So in the first day of creation, the Lords and Ladies arose from the chaos of night, and in that womb they deposited their love. From that seed of love burst forth the universe, as a flower bursts forth from a bud.

"The light of the First Creation spreads through the universe and creates life, for light carries with it the imaginative creative force of love. We owe our life on Earth to that light which permeates the universe. Creation is an act of love, a love present at the First Creation. We are the children of the love of the First Creation."

"Why do you pray to the Sun instead of to the Universal Spirit?" a man asked, a laborer on his way to work who had paused to listen to the prophet.

"A prayer to the Sun is a prayer to the Universal Spirit," Jalamanta answered. "In the annals of time, my soul is but a seed scattered by the cosmic wind. I am a brief spark that flares momentarily in this body. My soul partakes in the energy of Universal Spirit. I yearn to feel true union with the Universal Soul, but the Universal Spirit is large, encompassing, unfathomable. That which we call the Transcendent Other, or God, is immense and mysterious. That God remains an abstraction. But when I reverence the Sun, I can actually feel a reflection of the Universal Spirit."

"These are not the teachings of the moral authorities," an elder said. "Your words are an echo of the native teachings. In your Universal Spirit I sense the words of the early prophets. Do you not believe in God?"

"That which we call God is an abstraction that cannot be known. Therefore, the transcendent power in the universe is known by many names. We yearn for a deity that is personal and close, a god interested in our affairs on Earth, so we create gods in our image. We create gods to fit our needs, and those gods reflect our humanity. The greater, transcendent power of the universe cannot be described in human terms."

The elders grew nervous. Jalamanta was saying

that the mind of God could not be known. The faculties of men and women could never really describe God.

"Since the light of consciousness filled our ancestors, millennia ago," Jalamanta continued, "we began to contemplate the mystery of life. It is natural for us to wonder about the creation and the creator. Survival has made us inquisitive. Our souls do partake of the original creative imagination. So we have created the spirits of wind, fire, mountain, ocean, and rivers. We even have imbued the animals with aspects of the deity. For some the Mother Goddess became our creator. On and on it went. Through the ages we have created gods in our own image.

"Later, we called the creator of the universe Lord, and we ascribed our desires to that god. The desire for communion with a personal god is so strong we created an image of the creator and imbued it with our characteristics. By making the Universal Spirit personal, more immediate, we felt closer to the transcendent consciousness of the universe.

"Throughout our evolution we have created gods, and we have held each one up as the true god. But each of those gods has disappeared in the sands of time. Only the true light of the First Creation remains constant."

"Are you returning to the old religions that worshiped the Sun?" a man asked.

"I lift my arms to the Sun and ask that its light

bless all of life. I have great reverence for this star spun from the First Creation. Our Sun reflects that divine coming into being of the universe. I cannot know directly the mind of the Universal Spirit, but when the light of the Sun bathes me, I feel the Universal Spirit filling me. The energy of the Sun nurtures body and soul; it nurtures the Earth. My prayers are to the Father Sun, the Mother Earth, to all of life. My prayers rise to the expanding consciousness of the universe."

"You say we cannot know the transcendent God," the man said.

"We can meditate on the nature of that transcendent consciousness which is the universe, but I do not clothe the Universal Spirit in the body of man or woman," Jalamanta answered. "When we stand in awe of the universe, or when we experience a crisis in life, we understand the need we have to pray to a Father God, just as in prior times when we spoke to a Mother Goddess. But when we clothe the Universal Spirit in human terms, we limit the nature of that ever-expanding consciousness. I am a man of this Earth. This light within is all I know of God."

A young man who had listened very intently stood up. He was an artist who yearned to paint the colors of the fields, the faces of his people, but the only work available was in the industry that dealt with the transmission of images and which was controlled by the central authorities. They controlled the channels of war and knowledge and thus controlled even the work of the artists.

"What you say is interesting," the artist said, "but it is only speculation. What good are words when we are struggling in the darkness. The alleys and streets are our home. Children sleep in the craters of bombs; they eat the leftovers of the rich. This prayer of yours is a fantasy, the dream of an old man. Our world is real."

"The Path of the Sun is real," Jalamanta answered. "Can you not feel its warm light nourishing you at this very moment? Can you not feel its light penetrating flesh and earth alike? Even at night the work of the Sun is not done; its energy emanates from everything it has touched. It is light that reveals the essence of reality!"

He became animated as he spoke, because what he felt within was a truth to be shared. He had no church, no cult, no following to bid to do his work. For those gathered around him, he only wished the clarity of the soul to be revealed.

"Share that essence with us," a young woman said eagerly, her soul weighed down by the violence and disorder of the world.

"Rise," Jalamanta said, and they rose. He reached out and offered his hands to Fatimah, and she too rose.

"Face the east," he commanded. "Hold your arms up and ask the Giver of Life to bless all of life. Allow the light to penetrate your soul. The sunlight that touches you is a reflection of the

First Creation. Through the light of the Parent Sun, you can join your soul to the Universal Spirit."

All were touched by his enthusiasm. They closed their eyes and raised their arms to the morning Sun, and the rays of the Sun warmed their faces.

"Bless all of life," they whispered, aware that for the first time in a long time they were asking for a blessing for themselves, their neighbors, and the Earth.

The aloneness that had kept each person separated from the others slipped away, and each felt the soul within shining with light. A new energy was created: the energy of their souls in communion.

The light filled them with peace and joy; their prayer became a song that connected one to the other. The essence of the mystery unfolding before their eyes created a sharing.

"When you open your soul to the clarity of light, you arrive at a new awareness. The essence within will be revealed, and its connection to the Universal Spirit will be revealed. This is the Path of the Sun," Jalamanta said.

"I feel the light," a young man said, his words full with the revelation. "It is all around me, bathing me in clarity."

"Offer the light within to the four directions of the Earth, so people may share in your clarity," Jalamanta spoke softly. "You are the center, as the First Creation is the center of centers. The directions meet in you, the colors of the four sacred mountains meet in you. The Cosmos meets in your soul."

Each soul opened to the clarity. Each shared in the simple mystery.

It was an ecstatic moment of contemplation, a brief epiphany that allowed each one a glimpse of the soul within. Around them, they felt every particle of life, living and not-living, touched by the shimmering light. Clarity revealed beauty, and each one was at peace.

Then the spell broke and the people turned to look at each other. Their faces radiated the beauty they had shared.

"Can this meditation be repeated?" one of the elders asked.

"Yes," Jalamanta replied. "You know the essence within, and it will reveal the beauty you need to make life meaningful."

The crowd pressed forward to thank him, asking him to come again the following morning. Now there was the work of the day to do, but their souls had been nourished by the moment. They desired to learn more of the Path of the Sun.

"We will follow your instructions, master," some said, reaching to touch him.

"You need no master," Jalamanta replied strongly. "I did not speak to gather a following. Each person cultivates his soul, and you yourselves are the community you seek."

Fatimah touched his arm. He had not yet fully recovered his health, and he gave so much to the people. It was time for him to rest.

He nodded, and together they walked up the river. In the morning light the water was a slate of silver, a shimmering of light.

"You must not blame the people," Fatimah said, responding to Jalamanta's concern. "They have been oppressed for so long that they need to gather around you."

"But I preach no cult," he answered. "It is in their power to create the community of souls. For that they need no master."

"They will understand," she said, and touched his arm.

He looked into her eyes, and the gaze of her love was like a calming balm. He smiled. "Being here with you, I am filled with the memories of childhood," he said.

"Memory seems to grow more poignant with time," she answered. "It was here that we made love long ago."

"I remember," he said, and gathered her in his arms.

Love filled Fatimah's heart. In his arms she was content, and still she sighed. There was a secret she had to reveal. She knew she would have to gather the strength to tell Jalamanta about their son. She knew the pain that he would feel when she revealed the past, the pain of never having known his son. Jalamanta sensed her thoughts.

"Together we felt the bursting of the bonds of aloneness," he said to her. "Together we first walked on the Path of the Sun."

"I have kept the promise we made when we were young," she said, and smiled. "My prayers have been like doves flying across the desert with the message of my heart."

Joy filled his soul. He had sent his thoughts to her, and she to him. Her dreams caught in the web of his dreams, and they filled him with hope.

"Those prayers helped me survive my darkest hours," he said. "Such is the power of the soul that it can take flight."

THE LOST
SON

That evening Jalamanta and Fatimah sat in the arbor outside her kitchen. The vines were heavy with clusters of ripe grapes. Around them the branches of the fig trees were bent with the weight of the small, dark figs.

They sat in the gentle twilight after their meal and enjoyed the sweet figs and goat cheese. Jalamanta was a man of the spirit, she knew, but he was also a man who relished the fruits of the earth.

"To eat is to absorb the energy of the fruits and vegetables," he said. "The brother fish we take from the river, or the deer from the mountain, give their breath of life to be incorporated into our breath. At each meal we are thankful."

In the dusk, even their silence was a communication. He, who had spent so much time away from Fatimah, had quickly grown accustomed to her rhythms. She, whose heart was full of joy, moved around him as if they had never parted.

They touched in passing, or he reached across to hold her hand in his, and the love they had known when young rekindled, as a flame grows from embers when the lover's sweet breath fans the heart of fire within.

Soon Santos and Iago would be coming up the trail to join them in the evening conversation.

Fatimah turned to Jalamanta. Today he had spoken of the First Creation, the love that was the seed in the womb of time. Now was the time to tell him of their son, how the seed he had deposited in her long ago had borne fruit. He should know from her so that he might not hear it unexpectedly from someone else.

Ah, but it was a sad story, one whose ending would bring pain to Jalamanta.

He felt her inquietude, because he asked, "Tell me what your eyes have kept secret from me all day."

"It is a story difficult to relate," she said. Her eyes filled with tears. "How different things would be if only—"

"We cannot change the past," he said, stroking her hair, sensing the sadness in her heart.

"If we could change the past, our son would be sitting here with us," she whispered.

"Our son?" he said, drawing close to her. Could

it be that the love they once shared had brought forth a son?

"Is it possible?" he whispered, an ache growing in his heart. He held her face in his hands and looked into her eyes.

"Yes," she nodded.

"Oh, joy," he exclaimed. "Now I understand why in my dreams I often saw a young spirit at your side. But where is he?"

"This is the part I dread to tell, and yet you must hear it from me. When he was eighteen, he was forced to serve in the military of the regime. He was reported lost in a battle."

"He's dead."

"The authorities refused to tell me if he is dead or missing. But I have hope he is still alive! Many times I feel him near me, speaking to me, and then I know someday he will return. . . ."

"Oh, my soul, give me strength now," Jalamanta cried, and gathered her in his arms. Listening to her heart beat, he knew the loss had been most painful to her. She had raised their son alone and felt the loss alone.

"I did not come in time," he sighed. "I was not here to help you."

This had been part of his dream. During those long years in the desert, his thoughts of Fatimah had sustained him, and he had seen a young man at her side, but he did not know till now how to interpret the dream.

"I told him about you," she whispered. "Each

evening we would sit here, as we are sitting now, and he would ask me about you. You would have been so proud of him. He was a good son, filled with an inner beauty."

"And I could not be here to share," Jalamanta said, and rose. He peered into the dusk. "I curse those who separated me from you, from him," he said in anguish, covering his face with trembling hands.

The true pain of the years of his exile was now evident. He had lost that time most cherished; his son had grown but not under his tutelage. Tears filled his eyes. Homecoming also held its bitterness.

By the river he heard the cry of the doves. The swallows of dusk swooped and flitted over the river in their mystic flight.

Fatimah went to him. "Don't curse those who are not worthy. I was happy to have him with me. His spirit is with us," she whispered. "Like you, he loved to roam up and down the river and into the hills. He kept a watch for you. At the end of the day, he would look across the desert."

"You have been strong," Jalamanta said. "If only I could have been here."

"You were with me in my dreams," she replied, "lending me strength."

"Now the doubts come to cover my soul. Should I have set out on this path? Should I have ever questioned the authorities?"

"It could be no other way," she replied, her voice comforting him. "We do not know the destiny of each soul on Earth, but we do know they are near when we have need of their strength."

Jalamanta nodded. Yes, the spirit of the son he had not known was near. That is why the swallows swooped so low, joyful in their flight. His spirit was with them. In the dusk their son was the darting bird that came to remind them that the soul did not die.

"Yes, he is with us, he is alive," he said to Fatimah, and together they sat in the evening light and enjoyed the flight of the swallows.

Their bond of love could overcome even the grief they felt.

PAIN AND SUFFERING

"Life is cruel and full of suffering," Iago said as he and Santos came up the trail to Fatimah's home to sit and talk.

"What pessimistic thoughts," Fatimah said, inviting them in. "Sit and I'll pour you wine to refresh your spirits."

"Ay," Santos agreed as they sat. "My friend Iago has grown to be a cynic. Today he is complaining of the gout that makes it difficult for him to walk."

"Life is full of suffering," Iago said, and shrugged. "Why should it be so? Look at my feet, swollen like the feet of an old man. I give to the poor and hungry. At the end of the year, I give away my old clothes. Why should I suffer?"

"It's not just his feet, it's something inside he won't share," Santos whispered.

"Suffering is inherent to the flesh," Jalamanta said. "It has its purpose."

"Bah!" Iago scoffed, cutting a huge slice of cheese and washing it down with a glass of wine. "Give my suffering to someone else."

"There's enough of that in the world," Santos said. "Why do we commit so many atrocities against our fellow man?" he asked, turning to Jalamanta.

"Because we separate ourselves from each other when we inflict pain," Jalamanta replied. "We make people objects and forget they possess a soul. Before I walked on the Path of the Sun, I blamed God for pain and suffering. Now I know that each one of us bears a responsibility for every other person on Earth."

"The flesh has its appointed time on Earth," Santos said, "and you're right, suffering is natural to us."

"Suffering is also natural to the soul," Fatimah said.

"I don't feel pain in my soul, I feel it in my feet," Iago complained.

"Don't be such a crybaby," Santos chided his friend. "Think of those suffering from war and hunger."

"If we allow it, pain becomes a veil that clouds the soul," Jalamanta said. "Robbed of its strength, the soul gives in to the suffering of the body."

Iago raised an eyebrow. "You think the pain is in my soul? If so, how do I cure it?"

"Pain can be used to create light for the soul. Our evolution toward a higher consciousness can use the energy of pain. Each of us turns inward when we are in pain, and in that turning inward lies a new awareness."

"Awareness of what?" Iago questioned.

"Pain and suffering are part of our growth into a new humanity," Jalamanta answered. "We see on Earth that everything has its appointed time. The fragile leaf and the highest mountain weaken and die, as the day is born, weakens, and dies. The very universe is expanding, only to turn inward, weaken, and die. Pain and suffering are part of the natural process of those eternal rhythms of birth, growth, and death."

"That sounds gloomy," Iago shivered. "You have no Lord God to blame for your pains, only this belief that pain is natural. What purpose does it serve?"

"No person should ever cause another person to suffer, for pain damages both body and soul. When we gather as a community, we will not allow one soul to hurt another. But the suffering that comes naturally reminds us to turn our attention within, for though the flesh prepares for death, the soul cannot die."

"When in pain, we are too weak and frightened to care for the soul," Iago contested. "That's how I feel now."

Jalamanta sensed his friend's inner anguish. He drew close. "One is never too sick to forget the soul. During time of pain we can turn to others for help. We are your friends and we can help." He reached out to touch his friend, but Iago shrank back.

"No one can help me. I am alone." He pulled into the shadows. He couldn't reveal the source of his true anxiety.

"If I cannot help, there are healers who can," Jalamanta said. "Wise guides who teach us how to turn pain into awareness. We help each other when we join in a community of souls."

Iago shook his head.

"Listen to him, Iago," Santos said. "There is no sin so great it cannot not be forgiven."

"You must start somewhere," Fatimah said.

Iago spoke. "You say if I go to this community of souls, they can lighten my pain. If I participate in the Divine Love of the Universal Spirit, then even pain and suffering have a purpose?" He laughed. He wasn't convinced.

"Aloneness creates distrust and turns us against each other," Jalamanta said. "When we do not believe in ourselves, we create the world of veils to keep us from knowing each other."

"No one is spared suffering and death," Fatimah said. "But we are all children of the Universal Spirit. Even our pain is part of that universal consciousness."

Jalamanta touched her hand. She understood. All those years in the desert, in solitude, speaking only occasionally to the scattered desert tribes, made it difficult for him to express the illumination he had found. He wondered if he was capable of explaining it to others. He grasped for metaphors, and yet he knew each person had to experience the inner clarity. No one could bring another person to the light and pour it into the soul.

"Pain and despair are real," he said. "Doubting myself drove me to despair."

"We suffer because of our original sin," Iago complained. "Suffering is atonement for the broken covenant of the first man and woman. By breaking God's commandment, we fell from grace and entered the world of suffering. So I suffer."

"So you believe in the mortification of the flesh," Fatimah said.

"Only by suffering can we be one with God."

"This world is an illusion, and so pain and suffering are illusions," Santos offered, happy that at last Iago was entering into the discussion. "Put away the Self and meditate on the Selfless. Pain will disappear. Suffering is the karmic retribution for our past lives. We are caught in the wheel of birth and rebirth, and as we sow in one life, so we reap in the next."

"Pain and suffering are a test of our moral strength," Iago said, shrugging. "God is just. I accept His punishment."

"No," Fatimah replied. "I have seen the devastation of our city. I lost my child to the war. I see people go hungry and homeless. How can this be the workings of a just God?"

"It is Jalamanta who crossed the desert who truly suffered," Santos said.

"Suffering is also a transformation," Jalamanta said. "And so I was transformed in the desert."

"How?" Iago asked.

"In the desert I met the sorcerers of doubt and despair," Jalamanta said. "Finding myself alone on the vast and dark plain, I doubted myself. I had no one to turn to, and the doubts became the demons that shrouded my soul."

Even now, even with Fatimah at his side, he found it difficult to talk about his crisis of faith. He knew now that when he gave up the old dogma of the moral authorities, he had given up the foundation of faith as it was written in the old laws. Once, he had trusted in those laws to answer the questions he asked, and when he found the answers lacking, he was not yet ready with his own. Despair and doubt engulfed him.

"But I have heard there is also a city of pleasure in the desert," Iago said. "Why not cover pain with pleasure. If I drink enough wine, I forget my pain."

"I came to that city," Jalamanta replied with a nod. "And there I was promised help by the sorcerers. They offered me all the pleasures of the city: drink, women, entertainment, food from faraway places, a world of stupor. I thought that by escaping into that orgy, I could erase the despair eating away at me. And yet the deeper I entered that world of false pleasures, the stronger my despair grew."

He paused. Fatimah touched his hand.

"Perhaps it was necessary for me to enter that labyrinth of darkness, for there I learned that the demons were within. The soul can exist in darkness, for it is indestructible, but it yearns for light."

"I don't understand." Santos shook his head.

"The soul is of the flesh and of the Earth," Jalamanta replied, "so it knows the darkness of the labyrinth of veils. In that darkness the monsters of doubt and despair become real. Each night the demons rose to haunt me, urged on by the sorcerers, who thrive on evil. There in that house of darkness, they broke my bones and left me for dead. They spread my bones and marrow on the desert sands. The dark night of the soul came over me. I died."

"You died?" Iago questioned. "A man cannot be reborn."

"The soul is constantly reborn," Jalamanta said. "The flesh dies, but the soul lives on. A kind healer found the center of my soul, that center of centers that cannot be destroyed. She brought me back to life."

"What is the dark night of the soul you speak of?" Iago asked. He had never questioned, and so he had never tested his faith.

"Questioning or denying the old scriptures brings on the crisis of faith," Jalamanta answered. "Some of the old tribes made God a father, a man of wrath and retribution. We have been taught not to believe in ourselves, but to believe in an image of a father. We place our trust in that image, but when we want to trust in ourselves, we are filled with despair. Too often we have not been taught to trust in ourselves."

"You have described the despair so many feel when they question their faith," Santos said.

Jalamanta nodded.

"Despair is that meaningless wandering in the desert. It is the labyrinth that has no exit. The soul needs a foundation on which to rest. Most accept the common teachings, placing their trust in images they truly don't understand. They never test the strength of the soul. I dared my soul to take flight, and not knowing the path, despair and doubt engulfed me. I roamed through the villages of the southern desert, and everywhere I saw the suffering of humanity. I came to understand that what we have in common is pain and suffering, and our mortality.

"Everywhere men and women struggle and chase after false desires during their brief time on Earth. We feel the frailty of the body, the ravages of war, the destructive turmoil of despair, the slow erosion of time. Then death comes and not an earthly trace is left. Even the gods of the past have died and been forgotten."

"Who were the sorcerers who broke your bones and left you for dead? Are these the minions of the Devil?" Iago asked.

Jalamanta smiled. Others believed in the demons, and believed that hell was a place where the demons resided and whence they came to plague mankind. Jalamanta knew the demons he had encountered were all of his own making.

"I created the demons who broke my bones," he answered.

"I don't understand," Iago said. "How can you create the very demons who came to destroy you?"

"By losing faith in myself, I entered the world of the dark labyrinth. By not trusting myself, I created the sorcerers who sucked the marrow of my soul. This is what the kind healer taught me. Doubt and despair are my own creation. We create our devils and demons. The mind creates its own haunting. Each of us must learn to care for the soul and fill it with light if we are to find the exit of the labyrinth."

"Who was the healer who helped you?" Fatimah asked.

"Memoria, a kind, old woman. She found me, found what was left of my soul. My soul was fragmented, bones tossed on the desert sand. Memoria's touch was healing. The people of the desert claimed she could fly, and I came to know she could. Some called her a shaman, a woman who heals fragmented souls. But she was much more than that. She is the guide who appears to us in our times of trouble, an old soul who knows the twists and turns of the labyrinth. She can point the way to the door of the light.

"'The unfolding of your soul is not yet done,'

65

she said. 'You have a role to play in its evolution. The Divine Love present at the birth of our universe has not yet come to its full fruition.'"

Jalamanta paused and looked toward the river, where the nighthawks and bats flew in the dusk. The chirping of the night crickets filled the air with a haunting melody. The booming sound of a frog sounded far away. The night was alive, as was the River of the Golden Carp, as was the river of stars flowing overhead.

"How fortunate you were to find that guide," Fatimah said.

"I don't like it." Iago shook his head. "There must be a better reason for our suffering."

"Other cults of the desert have taught this," Santos said to Jalamanta, "that a person can be healed by the laying on of hands, by surrounding himself with the prayer of friends."

Jalamanta nodded. He remembered his long nights and days of recuperation. The healer tended his broken spirit with prayers. Using her abilities and power as a healer, she taught Jalamanta how to gather his fragmented soul. First the healer listened to Jalamanta's story, then she prayed over him, talking to him all the time, giving him instructions on gathering the soul back to its center.

Jalamanta remembered and spoke. "The Path of the Sun teaches that the moment we turn toward the light for illumination, our soul becomes whole again. The strength for that flight resides within. The healer brought in members of her family and neighbors. When my soul could reach out and join in the community of souls, I grew stronger. I had conquered my aloneness and cast out the demons by gathering my fragmented soul. I had taken the first step on the Path of the Sun."

"Ay, and we are glad for that," Santos said. "You speak of the human touch that is healing. Tell us what you mean."

THE KISS
OF LIFE

Each of us can help the other, and oftentimes it is a simple reaching out and touching another's hand. The healer touched her forehead to mine, and that touching of the foreheads was a sharing that allowed the light within to tear away the curtain of despair. The simple touch," Jalamanta said in a soft whisper, "is the most healing act. It tells us that we are willing to share the energy of our soul with another. As helpful as science may be, one human touching another, one soul sharing its light with another, can restore the soul."

Iago stood. "In the city, science is god. All these things you say cast doubt on the rules of the central authority. You have not changed, Jalamanta. I say, be careful. Do not question so much. It can only lead to trouble. Good night," he said, and rose to leave.

"Oh, Iago, why are you so tormented?" Fatimah said, and reached for him, even as she suspected the secret that tore at him. But he drew away and disappeared into the darkness. They heard him hobbling down the trail, complaining as he went.

"He is the only one among us who makes money," Santos said, and also stood to depart, "but it cannot buy him happiness."

"If only he would share his torment with us," Jalamanta said.

"Perhaps it is so deep he can't," Santos suggested, looking at him. He knew of the jealousy Iago bore Jalamanta.

"The soul is never so shrouded with veils that it can't return to the clarity of light," Jalamanta replied.

Santos shrugged. "I believe you, but no one knows the soul of Iago. The people here along the river understand what you say. We have lived close to the desert since we were forced out of the city. We have listened to others who brought news from the desert. But we are few in number. Iago's right, those in power will not like what you say. The authorities have a chief inquisitor who questions those who deviate from their dogma. The inquisitor has come to rule our lives. People are dragged in and questioned without cause. Many have disappeared."

"It is so in many places of the world," Fatimah said.

"I must speak the truth I carry within," Jalamanta answered.

"Ay, that's what I'm afraid of," Santos said. He parted from them, pausing to touch his forehead to Jalamanta's and Fatimah's in a gesture of friendship. Then he too disappeared into the night.

"I must speak out," Jalamanta said when he and Fatimah sat alone in the cool breeze that wafted up from the river. "The healing of the soul is not only for me, it should not be a guarded secret. It is for everyone. The greater good lies in the community of souls."

"The light of your soul is the light of my soul," Fatimah said, drawing close to him. "I, too, was covered with veils of despair. First you were exiled, then our son was taken from me. But in my dreams the light of your soul shone on mine. I am afraid for you."

"It is the role of the inquisitor to instill fear in our lives. But we can put fear aside."

"And in its place our love will grow," Fatimah said.

She touched her forehead to his.

THE LORDS
AND LADIES
OF THE
LIGHT

The next morning Jalamanta rose to greet the sun. He and Fatimah sat in quiet meditation as the beauty of the new day washed across the desert and the river valley. Then the hungry goats brayed to be let out of the corral, and they drove the herd to the river.

"Here among the trees lives a presence," he spoke as they walked. "As a child I thought it was an evil genie, but I know now that the spirit of the place and the trees create a positive energy that is uplifting."

"So even the trees are your ancestors." Fatimah smiled. She knew the respect their ancestors had for all living things. Jalamanta was part of that tradition.

"Yes," he replied, "even the trees are imbued

with the light of the Sun. They, too, partake of the soul of the universe. They take the nutrients of the earth, water, and light and create energy, which is passed up to the heavens. Let's take our breakfast under the giant cottonwood. Remember when we were young, we often sat here?"

"I have forgotten nothing," Fatimah replied.

They let the thirsty goats hurry to the river while they sat under the tree and ate their cheese, figs, and bread. But even here people in the vicinity would not let them rest. They gathered around Jalamanta and asked him to speak.

"Tell us more of the morning prayers," one of the elders said.

Jalamanta spoke. "On a morning like this when the Sun rises to bless the Earth, it creates a dance of light. This is the dance of the Lords and Ladies of the Light. The Parent Sun, which our native neighbors call Grandfather Sun, is composed of the elements and light of the First Creation. It is a dispenser of the first light that stirred in the womb of time eons ago. The coming into being of the First Creation was a moment of imagination coming into consciousness, the birth of the Universal Spirit from chaos. It exists in our souls as a memory."

"How did that First Creation come to be?" one asked.

"All the tribes of the Earth have described that birth, because it is our birth," Jalamanta said. "In my meditations I have seen a spark lying nascent in the womb of time. In that formless chaos lies a positive and negative energy that is pure potential. Those energies are time and the 'light in time,' imagination and consciousness struggling to become. Their coming together is an act of Divine Love. The explosion of the First Creation is the coming into being of the consciousness of the universe. From the Universal Imagination we receive our creativity. From the consciousness of the universe we receive our knowledge. That first imaginative coming into being is divine because it gives birth to the light that will spread across the universe. It is divine because from that desire our souls are created within the bounty of the Universal Spirit. Our souls are a reflection of that light."

"The First Creation is what others know as God," one of the elders interrupted.

"The coming into being of the First Creation has many names," Jalamanta answered.

"Are you opposed to the old religions?"

Jalamanta smiled. "I am not opposed to religions or philosophies, unless they do violence to the peace and harmony of the soul. Unless they obstruct the evolution of the soul. I speak only of my path and the illumination I have found."

A young man stood to question Jalamanta. "You say our souls have memory of the First Creation, but we cannot even measure the eons of time that have passed since our universe first came into being. Man and woman did not walk on Earth. There was no Earth. How can we have a memory of an event millions upon millions of years ago?"

"Our souls reflect the light of the First Creation, so there abides a soul memory," Jalamanta answered. "Our soul energy emanates from the First Creation, as does the vital energy of the universe."

"But even the stars live and die," the young man said.

"But the light of the First Creation never dies," Jalamanta answered. "It is transformed, but it does not die. The light of our Parent Sun and the light of all the stars create the eternal movement of the universe. The people of the southern desert tell stories of suns that have lived and died. Four prior ages have existed on Earth, and thus they have marked the evolution of our kind. They call this the Fifth Age, and they call the Sun, the Sun of Movement. Now this age moves toward fruition."

"But there is violence everywhere. Will our time end in violence?" a worried woman asked.

"I listened to the prophets in the southern desert, and as bound as they are to the movement of time, they understand that the ending of an era is a struggle between the forces that keep the universe in tension. The creative light seeks harmony; the forces of violence seek destruction. We reflect that constant struggle, but we can choose the path of beauty and peace, the path of harmony with our neighbors."

"Is that what the Lords and Ladies of the Light teach?" Iago asked.

He had spent the night watching Fatimah's

house, and that morning he followed the two to the river. Even now he was consumed with jealousy. All his life he had desired Fatimah, and now Jalamanta had returned and Iago saw that Fatimah loved him.

He looked at Fatimah and wondered if Jalamanta knew the secret in his heart. Did he know of the deep jealousy he had harbored all these years? Would the Lords and Ladies of the Light reveal his desire?

"The Lords and Ladies are the light of the Sun. When the light shines on your soul, you take the first step toward clarity," Jalamanta said. "Allow the Lords and Ladies of the Light to fill your soul. Allow the clarity to enter."

The crowd looked at the beauty of the brilliant morning. The light shimmered on everything it touched. They stood in awe as the beauty of the new day washed over them.

Those who felt the light reflected in their souls understood. They stood transfixed in the presence of the shining light. The soul was a white rose blossoming in the sun. Each heart was filled with beauty and clarity.

"Each of you reflects the other. All are made one in the clarity of light. Rise each morning and greet the Sun as you would greet a parent you love," Jalamanta said, "for it has come to bless life and to reveal the mystery of the universe."

A woman had raised her arms to the dazzling display of morning light, and now she stood radiant.

"It is comforting," she whispered. "Through this simple prayer and meditation I can dispel the doubts that have clouded my vision." Her face was serene and glowing with an inner peace.

"She is a prostitute," a man shouted at Jalamanta. "She has no right to be here. She does not visit the house of God!"

"This is the house of God!" Jalamanta answered angrily. "You need no great cathedrals to live in the presence of the Universal Spirit. It is here. It is in your hearts! Look!"

He raised his arms and the people followed his gaze. They saw the glowing river, trees, the desert and mountain, the animals that walked upon the Earth, and the birds that had greeted the dawn.

In that dazzling moment desires were stilled. The quiet meditation on the beauty of the luminous light created clarity. Mind was imbedded in flesh, and flesh imbedded in mind. The soul was at the center. The soul was the unity of the miraculous mind and body.

The people grew calm, and the woman stepped forward to speak.

"I sell my body to exist," she said to Jalamanta. "Am I to be exiled from this beauty. Can I not walk on the Path of the Sun?"

"No one is exiled from the Path of the Sun," he replied. "The Lords and Ladies of the Light bring their clarity to all." He turned and spoke harshly to the man who accused her. "All souls are equal! All souls vibrate with the same essence of light!"

Then he touched the woman's forehead. "Open your soul to light, and you open your heart to love," he said to her.

"Your touch is soothing," she said. "The light enters and I feel the dark veils dropping away. I am part of this beauty you describe."

"You have broken the shell of the Self," Jalamanta said. "Once you were alone, distanced from others by your need to survive. You were driven from the community by those who are fearful and ignorant. Now the Lords and Ladies of the Light have opened your soul to the beauty around you. You can join the communion of souls. You can commune with the Cosmos."

"I thought I was not worthy," the woman said.

"The Path of the Sun is open to all," Jalamanta repeated. "There are no select or chosen few."

"Can it be true?" the woman asked. "When you are gone and I stand alone on a clear morning, will this magical moment fill my soul again?"

"Yes," he answered. "The prayers begin in the morning, but they may be said at any time. At the end of the day, the Sun shines on the Earth and creates another aspect of beauty. The Earth, warmed by the Sun, reflects the light it has absorbed. The Earth lights up like the love reflected in the lover's eyes. That is a time for contemplation, a time to gather the peace of the day within. This closeness you feel to life is the beginning of your journey on the Path of the Sun. Its simplicity has been known since the dawn of time."

As they would greet a newly baptized child, some of the elders pressed forward to greet the woman. They, too, felt the power and freedom of the baptism of light.

"Is this what the ancients of the east called meditation?" a young man asked, stepping forward. He had read many philosophies, and the ideas of Jalamanta intrigued him.

"It is a form of meditation," Jalamanta replied. "But the Path of the Sun requires no formulas or crafted dogma. Sitting or standing, alone or with friends, one simply allows the dance of the Lords and Ladies of the Light to enter. What I call meditation is the will of the mind slipping away and the soul shining freely. When I am filled with light, I feel connected to all of life. During those moments the soul is filled with illumination. The soul reveals its own memories and vision. Those moments are a communion of the soul with the light of the Sun and of the universe. The illumination dispels false desires. Strength comes from that communion, for the clarity of light comes to strengthen the soul."

"How is it the soul can grow stronger?" the young philosopher asked.

"Our time is full of despair and self-doubt," Jalamanta said. "We have forgotten how to care for the soul. In my travels I met many who yearned for a spiritual union to that which is transcendent. But their souls were clouded by veils, and so the yearning of the soul remained hidden from the light of the Sun. One has to strip away those veils and allow the soul to shine."

"Speak more to us of clarity," the young woman said. "Is it difficult to achieve this clarity? Does one suffer on this Path of the Sun?"

THE SOUL

Clarity illuminates the soul. Each of us carries within, the essence that animates life. Each of us is part of the essence that came into consciousness at the First Creation. The creation of the Cosmos was the expansion of the Universal Spirit's imagination, the creation of dream. Our souls are reflections of that imaginative birth that brought the first spark into consciousness. The stream of light in the universe is uninterrupted; it flows from the First Source outward, like a wind of light sweeping across the universe. Our souls are reflections of that consciousness, part of that cosmic wind."

"As you say, that light of the First Creation spreads throughout the universe," a man said, "but how can it be conscious?"

"For the glowing ember of the nascent spark to

ignite in the womb of time implies an imaginative force. The coming into being of the universe was spontaneous Divine Love. On Earth that love energy was to give birth to our humanity, so we share in that love. Like the rest of creation, we are in the process of becoming."

"We are born and die like stars," the man pondered.

"The form changes," Jalamanta went on, "the essence remains. While the soul rests in us, it is our duty to strip away the shadows so it may bathe in light."

"Can we see the soul?" a child asked.

Jalamanta picked a sunflower and handed it to the girl. "See how the golden petals shine with light. See the dark center that creates the seeds of propagation. See the roots that take nourishment from the earth and pass it to stem and leaves? See how the leaves reach toward the Sun. The soul may be said to be like a flower, growing upward, taking its nourishment from the Earth but reaching always for the light. You cannot see the essence that drives the plant, but you can see its beauty. Plants circulate the energy of the Sun as our souls circulate the love of the First Creation."

"I feel the soul within me as a ball of fire. Does the soul desire?" a man asked.

"The soul is full of desire," Jalamanta said. "It desires to understand its relationship to the mystery of the universe. It yearns for unity with the light of the First Creation."

"But if the soul is so powerful, why are we in conflict with ourselves?" the man asked.

"We create egos, and our egos create a distance between each other and the soul. The mind creates its aloneness. To feel we belong, we create families, clans, and nations, but even in these groups we often feel alone. This aloneness is an essential part of our humanity, but it need not dominate us. Love can break the shell of alienation. The soul desires to bond with other souls and create unity. Love is the true expression of our humanity."

"For me the spirit within seems to be an animal I cannot tame," another man said.

"The instinct of the soul is related to that primal world," Jalamanta answered. "We share the history of the Earth with animals. We are imbued with the same elements. Do not fear your instincts. Trust them to lead you to the soul. It is only the extreme instinctual or rational desire that shrouds the soul."

"But others have taught that the mind, our rational faculty, and the body are antagonistic. These dualities fight each other. Unity cannot be," a young man said.

"Mind and body are one in the spirit of light," Jalamanta answered.

A woman of great beauty stepped forward. "I have used the beauty of my body to please first this group, then that," she said. "I color my eyes, my lips, my hair, and I sculpture the shape of my bosom or my legs. I enjoy great popularity, but I am not happy. The reflection of my outer beauty is a rainbow, and I am applauded for that beauty, but I do not see that one brilliant light shining within. Will the mirror reflect my soul?"

"The beauty of your soul is reflected in your face," Jalamanta said. "Old or young, rich or poor, beauty is reflected in the eyes and face of the person. But the soul knows no vanity. It resides in the temple of the body, but it knows the flesh is temporary. The true mirror of the soul is the beloved."

"For me the soul is a dream that speaks to me at night," a young woman said thoughtfully. "It fills me with longing and passion."

"The soul is passionate," Jalamanta said. "Its passion is for clarity. It yearns to see directly into the nature of things. It yearns to strip away the veils that cover the mystery of the universe. The soul permeates the body, and so it finds fulfillment in the flesh. The sense of being alone is dissolved in the passionate love of two souls."

"It is a restless spirit I cannot control," a man said.

"Without peace and joy the soul is a restless spirit, pulled this way and that by desire. In dream and memory the soul flies in search of peace. In its flight it encounters many other souls, and it shares their dreams. You cannot cage the soul, but you can learn to focus its energy so it will continue on the Path of Light."

"My soul is the love I feel within," a woman said.

"Yes, the essence of the soul is love," Jalamanta answered. "The path of clarity leads to love, for the coming into being of the universe was an expression of love. To speak of the First Creation is to speak of love."

A doctor of philosophy now stepped forward. He had listened to the discussion, but he kept quiet. Now he spoke. "There is no soul. Science has killed the soul. Why not admit that we are mere machines of flesh, animated by nerves, chemicals, and electro-rhythms. We become dust and a handful of useless elements when we die. God, heaven, and hell are only the fantasies of those who have nothing else to do but write down what they claim is the word of God."

Those of like mind nodded. Science had created machines to measure the universe. The unifying theory of physics was the only god possible, and that could be expressed in a mathematical equation. Science now knew each part of the body, and its constituent acids and proteins. Science could feed the mind chemicals and correct imbalances. But science had not found the soul, and what it could not measure did not exist.

"Science cannot find the soul because its light is the light of love," Jalamanta said. "So science renounces the soul. As to heaven or hell, they exist if you will them so. My life is bound to the Earth and its people, and so by crossing the desert, I created my own heaven or hell. I have seen the worst atrocities of men and women, and I have seen their noblest acts."

"You have seen the worst atrocities, and you still

believe we are inspired by a soul?" the philosopher asked.

"I did not set out to prove the existence of the soul," Jalamanta answered, "but what I found tells me I share in the vital energy of the universe. The essence within that resonates to the clarity of light is what I call the soul. A yearning in me seeks a clarity beyond the clarity of the mind's knowledge."

"And what comes with that clarity?"

Jalamanta paused. Should he tell them that the purpose of clarity was to become God? Were they ready to hear that the person on the Path of the Sun was filling the soul with light, and that was the path of becoming God?

Later I will speak of the ultimate quest of the soul, he thought. Now I will speak of good acts and how we can help each other in this difficult time of transition.

GOOD ACTS

A soul that admits light and trusts the essence of its nature will perform good acts for its neighbors and for the Earth."

"Is that all? Good acts?" the doctor of philosophy laughed. "Why, I expected you would reveal the mystery of life."

"The mystery of life is revealed in contemplation," Jalamanta answered calmly. "When I am filled by the Lords and Ladies of the Light, I feel the ecstasy of clarity, and clarity reveals the good acts we must perform to create the new era. Some think the transcendent mysteries are revealed only to mystics, but I say the everyday poetry of life and the stream of light that bathes the Earth, all these simple things can be used imaginatively by the soul to fulfill its yearning."

Some women in the crowd nodded. They understood his words. They had felt the poetry of life in giving birth, in providing for family, in their work. The soul revealed itself in such things. Yes, the laws of science and the thoughts of philosophers revealed parts of the mystery of the universe, but the mystery of the heart was revealed in intimate relationships.

"Yes, the new era should be one in which our actions are guided by the goodness in our heart," a woman said. "Or else we lose hope in ourselves."

"A cycle of time is dying," Jalamanta said. "Now we ourselves must create the new time on Earth. Yes, we must create a time of peace and understanding through our good acts."

"But isn't action contradictory to contemplation?" a man asked. "I have heard that only the soul at rest can be illuminated. Scurrying here and there creates confusion."

"The mystic soul loves its moment of meditation. To be infused by the Lords and Ladies of the Light is to become one with the transcendent universal consciousness. But being attentive to the soul does not mean one withdraws from life. Our good acts move humanity to a new plane of consciousness, where it may flourish. The essence within seeks illumination, and that same light drives our actions."

"And what are these good acts?"

"To love each other," Jalamanta answered.

Many nodded in agreement.

"Other prophets have taught this commandment," the doctor of philosophy said, "but it doesn't work. By our nature we are greedy, acquisitive, and egotistical. Each of us wants what we can accumulate for ourselves. In short, we desire power over others! Your idea of a new humanity is a dream."

"Those who preach distrust keep us separated from each other," Jalamanta answered. "We have been taught not to trust ourselves and to surrender our will to others. Thus others come to control our thoughts and actions. Those in power manipulate our loss of self-trust and teach us to hate others. We must learn anew that each soul is like the other. The change will not come overnight, but it will come."

Natives from the outlying villages in the hills had come to listen to Jalamanta. A child from one of the groups stepped up and took Jalamanta's hand.

"Do I have a soul?" the child asked.

Jalamanta lifted the child for all to see. "Yes. In your face I see your soul reflected," he said. "The light of the Sun shines in your eyes. You are a child of the First Creation."

He handed the child to Fatimah and turned to the crowd. "The soul is like a clear crystal with many facets. Each facet is an ego, a unique part of our nature imbedded in the flesh. When the egos are united, the soul shines with all its brilliance, as it shines in this child. At the center the pure light of the First Creation is gathered. But egos are created by desires, and they distort the light. As a diamond reflecting the light of the Sun creates a rainbow of colors, the soul's light may be squandered in colorful egos. A divided soul tugs and pulls at the person, seeking fulfillment of first this desire, then another. Each color considers itself the most beautiful, and so the egos run rampant. Still, the restless egos yearn to be reunited with the center."

The people who sat around Jalamanta thought on his words, and in the silence a young man spoke.

"I have felt distrust of myself and others," he said. "And I understand how the central authorities have used that weakness in me to serve their need to stay in power. By making me feel I stand alone, they create division, and that breeds the violence we see. It is time to take back our power! I will do good acts, and I will treat my neighbor as myself, but I feel there is more not yet revealed in your words."

The elders nodded. One man stood. "Speak more of the soul," he said. "What is its goal?"

BECOMING
GOD

Jalamanta looked at Fatimah. Now is the time, her clear eyes said.

He bowed to her, but still his heart questioned: Would they understand that the soul is the Holy Grail filled with love and light, and that in seeking unity with the Universal Spirit, the soul was becoming God.

"To open yourself to the light is the first step toward clarity of spirit," Jalamanta said. "As we mature, our minds become veiled with shadows. The material world weighs heavy on our souls. We forget that even the world of matter is vibrant with light. Our mind creates egos and they are filled with desire. Those excessive desires become entities, shadows of desires. They shroud the soul. We must learn anew to see into the true essence."

"How do we learn to see?" a man who had been wounded at war asked.

"Seeing is stripping the veils away," Jalamanta said. "When you can see the light shining on a dewdrop or stone or blade of grass, you are no longer separated from the world. When you can turn to your neighbors and greet them as yourself, you are revealing the beauty of the light within. The same energy of the Sun that creates life and fills your spirit imbues everything. You must become one with the Universal Light."

"I have such a yearning," a woman said, "but I have not understood it. I have felt empty and cold inside, and the world is also empty and cold."

"The soul yearns to be filled with light," Jalamanta said, "but in this age of shadows, we have weighed it down with illusions. We have created this separation between matter and spirit, when in truth the Universal Spirit permeates everything. The soul yearns for harmony, and there can be no harmony if it remains separated from the unity of life. The soul yearns for peace, and our egos struggle against others and create violence."

"But to desire harmony and peace is also a false desire," a young practitioner of meditation said. "I meditate on nothingness, and I arrive at nothingness. This is the nirvana taught by the masters of the East."

"I do not teach putting the power of the mind aside," Jalamanta replied. "The mind is an ally of the soul. They are composed of the same energy, they yearn for the same clarity. When the illuminated soul is full of the passion of the Universal Light, the mind understands the unity of creation."

"You speak of the passion of the soul," a woman said. "Before we were taught that the soul was lifeless, a spirit not interested in the world. I feel this yearning you speak of. I feel a passion in my soul."

"It is the passionate soul that seeks the light," Jalamanta said. "Mind and soul become one entity in the process of being filled with light. When the soul and mind are integrated, they move as one. Harmony and peace are a natural outcome of that awareness that joins us to the expanding love of the First Creation. We move toward unity with the center."

"And that unity takes humanity to a higher consciousness?" the woman said thoughtfully.

"Yes," he replied, "as the soul fills itself with light, it is becoming God."

An anxious ripple coursed through the crowd. Man and woman becoming God? What did the prophet mean? Was this the heresy the central authorities accused him of?

"As the soul fills itself with the light of the First Creation its fusion with the energy of the universal consciousness is complete. The soul filled with light has become one with the Universal Spirit."

A hush spread over the crowd. The elders strained to listen. Had they heard correctly? Did

Jalamanta say each person was becoming one with the Universal Spirit? How was this possible?

"We have not understood you," one of the elders spoke, an old man bent with age. He had read the scriptures all his life, and he listened attentively to all the desert wanderers who came to preach. In his heart he sought God, but the scriptures said the communion he sought was possible only when the soul departed the body at death. And then the soul remained an entity unto itself, enjoying the pleasures of heaven, but nowhere did the old scriptures say the soul became God.

"We can be with God when we die," he said. "Is that what you mean?"

"The soul that opens itself to light will become one with the energy of the Universal Spirit. As the veils are pulled away, the soul is participating in the light of the Universal Spirit. It is becoming God. We commingle with the Universal Spirit."

"For those who have led a good life, this is possible," the elder said. "One dies and the soul flies to God."

"One need not die to join the spirit of light," Jalamanta said forcefully so his words would not be misunderstood. "To walk on the Path of the Sun is to seek unity. Body, mind, and soul can feel the infusion of the light of the First Creation. To become one with the Universal Spirit is to become that light. That unity is possible here on Earth. Look at the plants, the river, the mountain, and all the animals. Already they are filled with light and are one with the consciousness of the universe. We, too, may be filled with that light and not die, but go on living with the divine spark illuminating our path."

Ah, the elders nodded and looked at each other. This is what the old stories meant when they told of men and women who had eaten God. They became one with the Transcendent. The mystics, those holy people of old who sought clarity, and those called saints and prophets all had been filled with light and become one with the All Encompassing. In their caves and monasteries they felt the ecstasy of God. The veils of the world were stripped away, but those mystics filled with God did not die.

"What you are saying is blasphemy!" a man cried from the back of the crowd and approached Jalamanta.

The people turned and looked at the representative of the central authorities. His name was Vende. He dressed in a brown uniform and black boots. On his cap was sewn an insignia of three skulls.

The people of the neighborhood knew his job was to snoop and report back to the chief inquisitor.

"Heresy!" he cried. "Man cannot become God!"

He turned his anger on the crowd. "This man is a false prophet! Be careful you are not misled by him! What he preaches goes against the dogma of the moral authorities! You know that!" He pointed at the elders. "And yet you allow him to speak!"

"He is free to speak," one of the elders protested.

94

"I will mark that," Vende fumed, making a note in the notebook he carried. "As for the rest of you, I warn you to disperse, or I will be forced to call the guards!"

"We are doing nothing wrong," the elders resisted. "It is our custom to welcome all desert travelers and allow them the forum to speak. Jalamanta has served his time in exile, and we will listen to him."

"You are fools!" Vende trembled in anger. "You will answer to the authorities!" he shouted at Jalamanta, turned, and left, making his way up to the road that led to the guarded gate of the city.

Fatimah touched Jalamanta's hand. "Vende will report you to the central authorities."

"But the elders have said I have a right to speak," Jalamanta said.

Santos, who was nearby, also stepped forward. "There are some who cannot be trusted," he said. "Listen to Fatimah. Come away."

But the crowd would not let Jalamanta leave. His words had created excitement. The elder who had questioned Jalamanta spoke again: "What you say allows everyone to commune with the light of the universe. Other prophets have said we must die before we gain heaven. Some say the Transcendent can only be achieved by a chosen few. You have opened the door to everyone. We must hear more of this."

"Yes," Jalamanta said, "the door is open to all. When we realize we are capable of communion with the light of the Universal Spirit even as we walk on Earth, we begin to understand our humanity. When we have bonded to the cosmic spirit of love, we can open our souls to greet every person as ourself. Then we will truly create our humanity."

"The truth is within," one of the elders murmured.

"Truth, beauty, inner peace, and all that relates us to the Universal Spirit is within, waiting to be acknowledged and revealed. Our souls are a reflection of the First Light. The Lords and Ladies of the Light are also a reflection of that First Light. When you allow them to shine on your soul, they will reveal the truth you carry within.

"I have spent a lifetime on the Path of the Sun, and each day is a new illumination. The soul within is as large as the Cosmos, and what is revealed daily is the mystery of life itself. The soul can never be filled with too much light. Each day is a step toward clarity, each day one learns to see deeper into the nature of the universe."

As he spoke, the full beauty of the morning blossomed, like a flower of the Sun opening its golden petals. Those gathered around Jalamanta felt the blessing of the Sun. The Lords and Ladies of the Light penetrated everything with their dazzling dance, and all of life was for that instant connected. The shadows dissolved, and the unity created was a sacred moment of transcendence.

THE DANCE
OF LIFE

The Earth is alive!" a young woman exclaimed. "The light creates the dance of life!"

She was a dancer who taught the children the joy of dance. But she had not felt the dance of light until that morning. Now she felt everything around her swaying to the rhythm of the Lords and Ladies of the Light.

"Yes," Jalamanta said, smiling. "It is the dance of life."

"Can anything be as beautiful as this?" she exclaimed, her eyes open for the first time to the shimmering of the Cosmos.

"You and your dance are that beauty," Jalamanta replied. "The soul is a creative energy. The illumination of clarity brings joy! Dance!"

The young woman turned to the young man

who accompanied her. He lifted his flute to his lips and played a light, airy melody.

"Come!" the dancer said and pulled her friends into a ring. "Let us dance! Let us dance and greet the day!"

The children jumped to their feet, but the elders held back.

"Do not hesitate!" Jalamanta cheered the young woman. "Dance as the Lords and Ladies of the Light dance! Lift your spirits and join each other in this dance of joy!"

He turned to Fatimah, and she took his hands. They joined the circle of dancers. Side by side they danced, feeling the warmth of their souls uniting, feeling love in the touch of their hands, love in the greeting of their eyes.

Others stood and danced, cautiously at first, then with the gusto instilled by the melody of the flute and the good feeling between neighbors. Some assisted those crippled or blinded, until all joined the circle, swaying softly in the light.

In their bare feet the children danced, and as they sang and laughed, they spun around in a wide circle, like the swaying plants and trees in the luminous light of morning.

When they were done, they fell on the grass, exhausted but full of joy. "Every morning I will dance this dance," the young woman proclaimed with a smile.

"We will dance with you," the children said.

"There can be no greater gift than to express the joy of the soul," Jalamanta said.

"Bah," a man complained, "dancing is for those who have nothing else to do! Dancing doesn't feed my family. I have work to do."

He had come because he was intrigued by Jalamanta's words, but he had not joined the dance. He was too busy thinking of opening his shop for the day's business.

"Seeing is not learned in one day," Jalamanta replied. "The world calls to you. The action of life is necessary in the world, for life expresses itself in movement. But you can learn to carry the light within even in the most pressing of circumstances. It will sustain you, guide you, and the movement you thought was only a play of shadows can be the play of light."

"What must I do?" the man asked.

"You must be attentive to your soul," Jalamanta replied. "The soul that is not daily filled with light will wither and die. You know that if you do not take care of your business, it will not profit. If you are not attentive to your soul, nothing will profit you. Go in peace. Walk in clarity."

"Thank you," the man said, "I will try. Every morning I will devote a few minutes to this clarity you talk about. In the meantime, I have to work to feed my family."

The people understood that the movement of life was the surface of life, and penetrating all was the essence of light. The veils were illusions to be stripped away to reveal the true scintillating light.

"Will you speak more?" the people asked.

"I will speak tomorrow," Jalamanta answered, "but now, as you can see, we must tend to our goats or there will be no milk tonight."

He gestured to Fatimah's goats, which had wandered on down the river, browsing in the thick bushes.

"Ay," one of the elders nodded, and turned to address the crowd. "So must we all tend to our work. We will gather here in the morning and listen further to Jalamanta."

The crowd dispersed, and Jalamanta followed Fatimah.

"The people hunger for knowledge of the spiritual path, and yet they are fearful," he said.

"Yes, they fear the guards of the central authorities. They have imprisoned many of our elders who spoke of the old traditions. They will not allow you to go on speaking as you have today."

"And Vende is one of us," Jalamanta said.

Fatimah shrugged. "Like others, he has put on their uniform and now makes his living snooping and passing rumors about our activities to the authorities. But he is a fool. There are more dangerous spies in our midst."

"Who?"

"Those very people you described. Those whose souls are clouded by false desires."

"Is there someone you suspect?" he asked.

"Your old friend," she replied softly, and looked toward the thicket where a shadow lingered. It was Iago. When Jalamanta turned in his direction, Iago disappeared.

Could it be, Jalamanta thought, that an old friend would break his confidence? And yet he knew the false desires of the heart were real—veils that clouded the soul.

"Does Iago know the inquisitor?" Jalamanta asked as they led the goats out of the thicket and up toward the hills.

"Yes. And so do you."

"Who is he?" Jalamanta questioned.

"Benago," Fatimah answered.

Jalamanta paused. "The same Benago we knew in childhood?"

Fatimah nodded. "He worked his way into power, sparing no evil deed to get there. It is he who is responsible for our exile from the city. He and others took power, and the power corrupted him. He has put to death those he cannot manipulate."

"Ah," Jalamanta sighed. He knew this was the way of the world, but he did not want to believe that someone he knew as a child, even a child as mean as Benago had been, had grown to be a murderer. Yes, the age of violence was created by men and women who separated themselves from others. Those hungry for power grew more dangerous as they grew stronger. In their ultimate aloneness they turned on the humanity that had suckled them.

"I need to talk to Benago," he said.

Fatimah shuddered. She had known in her heart that sooner or later the authorities would take Jalamanta in for questioning or, as it came to pass, he would go and challenge them.

THE
SUMMONS

That evening a letter was delivered to Jalamanta. The courier was Vende, and when Fatimah saw him, she shivered. She knew the authorities were summoning Jalamanta.

"You must come immediately," Vende said. "The letter is signed by Benago himself."

"I'll go for Santos." Fatimah reached for her shawl. "Perhaps if he goes with you—"

"I am to deliver only the man called Jalamanta," Vende said coldly. "But do not worry. If they meant to keep him, they would have sent a detail of guards." He smiled dourly.

"I have nothing to fear," Jalamanta said, and embraced Fatimah.

The warmth of her embrace surprised him. He had felt her touch when she tended to him, and during the past few days, he felt a constant joy in her presence. Often, when she sat by him, he had felt the urge to hold her, as he held her now.

He looked into her emerald eyes, dark jade in the dim light. How many times had he dreamed of her eyes. How many times had the beauty of her face haunted his dreams. Now, as he held her, he felt the vibrancy of their young love flow from her.

He touched his lips to hers. "I'll be back. I promise."

Then he turned and followed Vende. They left the river and followed the main road into the city. At the gate of the city, the guards waved them through.

It was dark as they entered the walled city, a labyrinth of streets and alleys. To reach the center of the city, they followed narrow, winding streets. During the day, peddlers from throughout the vicinity came to sell their wares in the streets and in the small shops, but at night the city was deserted. Occasional shadows crossed the streets. These were the homeless and hungry, who had no place to go. From a lighted window came the laughter of a woman.

"What's that?" Jalamanta asked.

"One of the brothels, run by the state," Vende said as they passed in front of the place.

Soldiers lounged outside.

Ay, no wonder people prefer the river, Jalamanta thought. The city was gray and threatening.

Once, it had not been like this. The Seventh City of the Fifth Sun had been a center of commerce. People came from all over the world to visit its museums. Art flourished. Jalamanta remembered music, festivals in the parks, scholars presenting lectures.

Then the wars came, and a wall went up around the city. The central authorities declared war on their neighbors, and money went to buy war materials, not to educate the youth. The central authorities consolidated their power, expelling those who opposed them, using dissidents as scapegoats.

Now, the streets seemed foreign to him. Perhaps the weapons of war and the soldiers at every corner disoriented him. Gray smoke rose into the pale sky. In front of them rose the tall, ominous towers of the citadel.

Here in the dark tower in the center of the city, the central authorities ruled. Their power was now absolute. It had happened so quickly, Fatimah had told him. One day a democracy had flourished, the city was busy and vigorous, then next it was closed and in the hands of a select few. The generals and their inquisitor ruled with a heavy hand.

At the central door of the dark tower, Vende had to show his pass. Only the select few with state errands could enter this building with three skulls engraved on the steel door.

"Benago has sent for this man," Vende explained, and the guards let them pass.

So, Jalamanta thought as the giant steel doors opened to allow them entry, let's see how this bully from my childhood has come to be the inquisitor.

A long hallway led to the reception room. The flags of the central authorities hung on either wall, the white of the three skulls leering from the red background. The fine woven carpet beneath their feet had been woven by enslaved children, a tribute from an eastern potentate.

They entered a dimly lit room, and Vende ordered Jalamanta to sit. He pointed to the stool in the middle of the room. Jalamanta sat, and the courier disappeared. Opposite him stood a kingly chair and a table with a sheath of papers on it. Over the chair hung an awning embroidered with the three-skull insignia.

THE
INQUISITOR

After a long wait, a door opened and Benago walked in. Dressed in a black uniform with gold epaulets on his shoulders, he carried himself like a fat cock.

Yes, it was Benago, he who as a child had played war games and led the other neighborhood bullies in raids against the natives whose villages dotted the hills. "They are strangers who don't follow our way of life," Jalamanta remembered Benago inciting his friends. And so the seed of hate was sown at an early age. The young boys who followed Benago never stopped to question.

So while the other boys attended school, Benago's thugs joined the city militia that was consolidating power. By preaching hate, he rose in power. He had grown corpulent, with sagging jowls and a thick chest. His weight was due to overindulgence, but he strutted in the uniform of the chief inquisitor, creating the illusion of authority.

"Benago, it has been many years—" Jalamanta stood, but he was cut short.

"You are not to address me until given permission," Benago said harshly. "And then only by my title, chief inquisitor! Now sit!"

Jalamanta nodded and sat on the bench indicated.

"Are you the desert wanderer they call Jalamanta?" Benago began.

"You know who I am, Benago. We were friends. I remember—"

Benago held up his hand. "What you remember does not concern me. You have been summoned to answer questions related to your preaching. You are accused of heresy. You are here only to answer the questions I put to you! Do you understand?"

"I will answer as truthfully as my soul dictates," Jalamanta replied.

"Ah, the soul dictates," Benago mumbled and sat. "You must understand," he said leaning forward, "I have done you a favor by asking to see you alone. The generals wanted to question you. You realize," he said, his voice dropping to a whisper, "there are serious charges against you."

"What are those charges?" Jalamanta asked.

"You have gathered the people around you,

preaching false doctrines, telling them wild sto-ries." He fumbled with the papers on the table.

"I speak what's in my heart," Jalamanta answered.

"I have a written report, verified by witnesses, that you tell the people they are capable of becom-ing God. Do you really believe that?"

"Yes," Jalamanta replied.

Benago laughed, then coughed. "I was right, you have lost your mind! Your brains have been affected by the desert heat. Tell me how long were you in exile?"

"Thirty years," Jalamanta replied.

"And from whom did you derive these heretical ideas?"

"From my meditation. From the stories of the elders of the southern desert."

"They teach that a man can become God?" Benago sneered.

"The teaching I espouse is universal. Through-out history we have known that if we fill our souls with light, we participate in the Universal Light," Jalamanta replied.

"Yes, that's partly true. Our own moral authori-ties promise heaven to the masses, and it gives them hope, a hope we can manipulate. But go on, tell me more, then let me decide whether you should be tried for heresy." He paused and lit a cigarette. He was in control, and he was going to enjoy making Jalamanta squirm.

"My heresy is that I teach trust," Jalamanta said.

"I tell people to believe in themselves, to cast away doubts, and to walk on the path of clarity."

"What is that path?"

"It is the Path of the Sun, a way of arriving at unity with the Universal Spirit. By bathing our souls in light, we can transcend our limitations. We are part of a greater consciousness."

"And when a man arrives at this consciousness? Poof! Does he disappear?" Benago laughed.

"Quite the contrary," Jalamanta answered. "He is filled with the divine and vital energy of the First Creation."

"What is this First Creation? What does it have to do with the soul?"

"The soul's origin lies in the First Creation, so the soul seeks the love inherent in that First Light."

Benago scoffed. "What I know of people tells me they don't seek love, they want power and wealth."

"The deluded mind chases after false power," Jalamanta said, "but the soul's inner yearning tells it to seek enlightenment. The soul seeks the Unity of its origins. Our myths and stories all struggle to explain the origin, to explain our coming into being. These myths and stories of the Earth tell not only of our earthly home. Our soul's memory reminds us of our beginning. The stories also tell of the soul's journey."

"So, where is the soul going?" Benago asked.

"The soul seeks illumination. It consciously

recreates itself, and by fulfilling itself, it takes us to a new awareness of our humanity."

"But surely you do not believe that man can become God."

"The soul seeks unity with the Universal Spirit," Jalamanta repeated. "The soul in its journey is filled with the Universal Spirit, and to be filled with that clarity is to achieve true enlightenment. The elders of the desert called it 'becoming God,' and so I use their words."

"Nonsense!" Benago sputtered, and drew himself up in the chair. "I know the true nature of man! There is no soul, only a desire for power! Give up this nonsense or I will have you tried for heresy!"

"I will speak the truth," Jalamanta said.

"Blasphemy!" Benago shouted. He rose and pointed an accusing finger at Jalamanta. "If this is what you tell the people, then it is blasphemy! Man cannot become God! How dare you tell the unworthy they can become God! How can the worm we call man possibly become like God!"

"Doesn't your dogma teach we are made in the image of God," Jalamanta replied.

"That is a metaphor!" Benago responded. "Something to appease the masses!"

"Our words are metaphors that struggle to define the transcendent," Jalamanta replied calmly. "You describe your Jove-like figure as a thunderous old grandfather without compassion, a warrior, a bearer of lightning bolts. But that image is of your creation."

"It is the word of God!" Benago protested.

"It is the word of man," Jalamanta answered. "The Transcendent Other is beyond description. We join the light only by opening our souls to it. You say I am audacious for telling the people that their souls are in the process of becoming one with the Universal Spirit, and yet you claim to know the thoughts of God. You claim to have them written in books! No one knows the thoughts of the Universal Spirit. Only through the works of the creation can we describe the All Encompassing."

"Heretic!" Benago shouted, and fell into a coughing fit. He reached for the decanter on the table, poured a drink to calm himself. Then he peered at Jalamanta.

"I am sorry for you," he said. "You don't seem to realize the penalty for what you preach."

He paused, as if pondering his next move.

"I have tried to protect you. I insisted I speak to you alone. Yes, yes I am Benago, the childhood friend you once knew. And you are Amado, exiled for your first heresy. Ah, that was long ago, and I thought you would be a changed man. I chose to question you because I wanted to see you again. I wanted to see the man who has spent thirty years in the desert, searching for these ideas you call truth. I find you have not changed. I ask you one last time, recant. Put aside these wild ideas. I have great power. As the chief inquisitor, I sit at the head of the generals. Recant now and I can help you."

Jalamanta looked into Benago's cold eyes. No doubt he had great power. He could forgive Jalamanta. He was, after all, a childhood friend. Now was the time to decide.

"I can protect you only tonight. After tonight, I can do nothing. Do you understand what I am offering?" Benago said.

"I understand," Jalamanta answered.

"The generals received a full report of your activities. They are ready to try you now! And this time they would not release you in the desert. The prison and its tortures await you."

"But I cannot deny the path I've chosen," Jalamanta answered. "By allowing the light of the creation to enter my soul, I have been illuminated. By allowing the Earth energy to enter me, I have expanded my humanity. I have chosen the path of love."

"What you say is not written in the scriptures of the Seventh City!" Benago said.

"In the old days, every man had the right to preach his message to the people," Jalamanta said. "Now the old era of time is ending, and in this time of transition, a cosmic struggle is taking place between chaos and order. I have chosen the path of peace and harmony."

"So you do understand," Benago whispered. "This struggle is not only for the hearts and minds of men we would enslave, it's a battle of cosmic proportions."

"Yes. Each of us struggles on a personal level,

but our struggle also reflects the universal struggle between chaos and order. That is why I must speak out."

"It's too late to speak out. We have the power, and people understand power," Benago said. "You can change nothing."

"The true power resides in the soul," Jalamanta answered. "Your power is a veil that the people will strip away."

Benago shivered and drew back. Did Jalamanta believe that the power of the generals could be overthrown by the people? Such a belief was dangerous, for history had shown that when people believed in themselves, they could overthrow any ruler over them. A tremor passed through the folds of his body, and his face grew haggard.

"I fear you, Jalamanta," he admitted, the words a barely audible whisper in the huge room.

"I teach that we should not fear each other," Jalamanta said. "We can live under the rule of laws that are laws of trust. You threaten me because you fear me, and yet there is always time to reach out in peace."

Jalamanta extended a hand, but Benago drew back. His cold eyes peered into Jalamanta's. "I fear the revolution you preach."

"I preach love and trust for one another."

"Yes, it is the gathering of people who trust each other that we fear. When that fire ignites the hearts of people, not even our force can stop them. We know that, and that is why I fear you."

Benago knew he could neither sway nor intimidate Jalamanta. Even now, a serene beauty emanated from his face. They were the same age, and Jalamanta had suffered the exile of the desert, yet he seemed to have the strength of a younger man.

"Do you truly believe you are becoming God?" he whispered.

"Yes," Jalamanta nodded. "Others before me have been filled with light, and their good deeds have been recorded. The wise men and women of prior ages, prophets, those called the mothers of gods, the saints, holy men and women of all tribes, the elders who have walked on the path of light, all have become one with the light of the First Source. They have allowed their souls to open to the light. Filled with light, they preach of the love the soul radiates: Love one another and trust one another."

"Insanity," Benago said, "insanity. You wild prophets of the desert come to disturb the peace. Yes, we use might, but it is to institute order and keep the enemies outside our borders!"

"The soul knows no borders, and every man and woman is a brother and sister," Jalamanta replied. "When the soul radiates love, fear of others disappears. The soul, free of doubts and controls, treats everyone as equal. Once full of light, the soul can encounter and create a new humanity."

"Man is a worm, his life is filled with pain, suffering, death," Benago said weakly, afraid that if he let go of his beliefs, the words of the prophet would change him.

"I have seen the suffering of humanity," Jalamanta said. "The urge to control others brings out the worst in man. Rage, greed, lust, jealousy, and the demented urge to maim and kill are part of our history. It's the responsibility of each person to cast aside the veils of violence. As long as we blame our ills on a higher power, we take no responsibility."

"The people have given their responsibility to me," Benago said.

"Now we must take it back," Jalamanta said.

The two men fixed each other with determined stares. For Benago, Jalamanta had grown dangerous. His talks by the river were no longer innocent, philosophical speculation. He was determined to take back the power vested in the chiefs of state.

Jalamanta thought of the holy men of the southern desert. They had taught him that death was a natural event in the cycles of life. Men and women became enamored of the flesh, and they dreamed of immortality in their present form. They did not see the soul within, so they desired power over others.

"We understand each other," Benago said.

"Yes."

"But do you understand the power we wield? Do you know I can have you destroyed. You and thousands like you."

"And others will appear," Jalamanta replied.

Benago slumped back in the chair. "Yes," he muttered, "there is no end. We have set fire to the camps, and millions have died, and still new witnesses appear. Why? Why?"

"Because we teach the right path. Join us on the Path of the Sun," Jalamanta said again.

Benago shook his head. "It's too late for one whose hands are stained with blood."

"It's never too late," Jalamanta replied. "We do not judge. Each soul arrives in its own time to be filled with the clarity of light."

Benago stood. "I will not give up my power and authority."

"Your desire for power is a veil that covers your soul," Jalamanta said. "Once you desire power, distrust and hate grow in your heart."

"Yes," Benago acknowledged, "I can trust no one, so I must hold on to the power I wield. It is a cycle I cannot break. To trust means to give up power, and I will not give up the control I wield. No, I cannot. Go, our time is done. You are free for now, but I warn you, the generals are not yet done with you. If they come looking for you, do not turn to me for help."

With that he turned and lumbered out of the room. The door closed behind him; then the courier who had brought Jalamanta reappeared.

"Follow me," he said, and led Jalamanta down the large hallway and out the front door.

Fatimah was waiting in the street. "Thank the Great Spirit," she said, and gathered him in her arms.

A Dream
of Love

For a moment they stood in silence, holding each other in a tight embrace as the steel door shut behind them with an ominous sound.

"I was afraid for you," Fatimah whispered.

"There's nothing to fear," Jalamanta said. He kissed the tears that rolled down her cheeks. "Come, let's leave this place that is so shrouded by darkness."

Arm in arm they walked out of the city and down the road that led home. They entered Fatimah's small house, and together they prepared their simple supper. They ate goat cheese and the bread she had baked that morning, and while they ate, he told her of his conversation with Benago.

"You say we should not hold fear in our hearts," she said when he finished, "but I feared for you.

118

They will continue to hound you for what you say, and—"

He reached across and put a finger to her lips. "To fear for the loved one is natural," he whispered. "When I left with Vende, I did not fear for myself, but for you. I took your love with me into the desert, and yet I had not held you in my arms until that moment I left. Have I been so blind?"

"You needed the time to recover. And you have given so much to the people."

"And I have not held in my arms the woman of my dreams, nor tasted the lips that hold my truth. . . ." He rose and took her hands in his. "Will you share my bed tonight?"

She pressed close to him, letting his embrace be the Holy Grail she dreamed of. "Yes, I will share your bed," she said, kissing his lips. "I will share your life."

Together they entered the alcove. They lay down, and she covered them with the blanket she had woven for him.

"I have dreamed of your return," she said, her sweet breath a fragrance in the dark.

"I have dreamed of your love," he replied. "You were the Holy Grail I sought in the desert. During those long years I came to understand that the grail was the cup of your love. The image of the gold cup was the symbol of your soul, your love, the child you raised."

"The soul is that Holy Grail, and into it we empty our love," she whispered.

"The prophet said, 'when one's soul is full of love, the cup runneth over'."

"Our love runneth over," she said, content to be at his side, whispering in the dark, feeling the flow of love as ancient as the stars overhead, a commingling as natural as the river's flow.

Contentment filled Jalamanta. Fatimah's presence next to him was as intoxicating as the swirl of stars that could be seen through the arbor's branches. Up there a million stars danced with the light of the First Creation. The consciousness of the universe spread ever outward, growing in its capacity.

Here, next to him, the perfume of Fatimah's body was the aroma of rain on earth; her hair the fragrance of figs; her touch a warm excitement that made his blood tingle.

"Do you remember the day we first made love?" he asked.

"Of course." She smiled.

"Ah, time comes to rob us of so much," he said.

"Time robs the body, but not the soul," she replied softly.

He closed his eyes and felt the swirl of time around him, memories of his youth. He saw again the child Fatimah brought into the world. His child.

Time and her fragrance enveloped him, like the Lords and Ladies of the Light filling his body and soul with clarity. Time was one of the Lords of the Light, as death was one. Everything in the universe was bound by the Divine Love that could be felt in the heart.

What was time but the passage of light through the universe. What was light but Divine Love. The souls of lovers would be united, with the body or without. If there was a beginning, there would be no end.

The new cycle of time entering their souls was but a transition. There were many threats around them, but together they could cast out fear from their hearts. They could make the new era good.

The fragrance of love was sweet in the arbor, as sweet as the garden flowers of the patio, as magical as the night and its sweet sounds.

Fatimah moaned, a moan of love, and Jalamanta kissed her lips, the light and energy of his soul fusing with hers.

Peacocks called in the dark, a cry that echoed through the trees. The breeze in the trees was like the sound of the ocean surf.

Jalamanta remembered the grove of trees by the river where he and Fatimah met long ago. Their friendship had grown from one of children teasing each other to the tentative love of a young man and woman.

There in that secret grove they met and rested. They talked about the mystery of life, their desire to feel fully the essence of beauty around them. Then they slept. Side by side, they took their rest on the cool grass of the riverbank.

The river murmured as it flowed south.

Overhead birds sang. Goats and sheep browsed nearby; the soft tinkle of the bell on the goats told them all was safe.

Desire grew; they spoke of sharing their lives.

One hot day he had arrived before her, and the cool, sparkling water beckoned to him. He stripped and waded into the river to refresh himself. When Fatimah arrived, she stood in the shadows of the trees for a moment, watching him splash in the shallow water, hearing his laughter, in awe of his naked body and the brilliance of the water in which he splashed.

He was the water, he was the light. His body contained both. She undressed quickly and entered the stream. He turned and marveled at the beauty of her body, the sheen of her soft curves, her small, round breasts, the dark nipples like sweet fruits to be tasted, the mound of Venus and its silken hair.

For a moment they stood looking at each other, admiring the beauty of their naked bodies, feeling the throb of souls whose destiny was to be united in love.

He moved toward her and playfully splashed her with water, and she laughed and splashed back. She turned and ran, and he chased her along the shallows, the two of them splashing each other. The cascading light in a million droplets showered them.

Then, like one of the golden fish of the river, she dove into a deep pool; he followed. They swam in the depths of the currents with the golden carp of the river.

There in the deep, where the sunlight filtered through the water and created a screen for love, he caught her, and she turned and embraced him. Their lips met as they turned in the sunsplayed water, and they rose, exploding to the surface.

They gasped for breath, laughing, tenderly touching each other and feeling the excitement of the touch like a fire in body and soul, a flame to be satisfied.

The mood of the river was gentle, the sun a gold sheen on the surface. The large, golden carp of the river rose to the surface to swim in a wide circle around them, creating a mandala of love.

They held each other, feeling the sleekness of their wet bodies, breathing each other's warm breath, lips touching hesitantly, then warming as the tips of their tongues became hummingbird tongues sipping at nectar.

Arm in arm, they returned to the bank of the river, returning from the depths of the fish world, where they had been blessed by the water and the golden carp. Shivering, they rolled like lizards on the warm sand, like turtles seeking a bed of grass, laughing to the warble of the meadowlark's song. Soul joining soul, they entered each other.

Even now, he could feel her body against his. Soul and body becoming one. Man and woman united as one. He moaned, reached for her, felt again the curves of the woman he had adored.

And so it was that both Earth and energy and Sun light came to rest in the woman. That is what he had learned in her love, and that is where he had begun his quest. The first step on the Path of the Sun had begun with her love.

Love was divine then, as the First Creation was divine. The two souls reflected the love of the universe.

Yes, he remembered each moment as if it was carved in his heart, glyphs of a pleasant memory.

Oh, how sweet is memory. He moaned and opened his eyes. His heart was still throbbing from the ecstasy of love. Fatimah's fragrance lingered in the air, on the sheen of sweat that covered his body.

Ah, sweetness of life, he gave thanks. Yes, even in the night, the light of the Lords and Ladies kept its vigil. In the blood, in the heart, in each organ, on palms of hands, and on elbows and legs and head, the light was shining.

How mysterious and yet simple were the mystical times of life. Moments surrounding the soul, waiting to be entered.

He rose and touched the warmth of the blanket at his side, ran his fingers over the fine weave. He raised it to his nostrils and smelled the aroma, the perfume of sage that lingered in the warmth of her earlobes, the perfume of apples along the cleft of her breasts.

It is good to return home, he thought, rose,

slipped on his desert robe and walked into the kitchen. Fatimah looked up at him, a blush on her face.

"You slept soundly."

"It's the magic of the blanket." He smiled, went to her, and kissed her forehead.

"I'll fix breakfast," she said.

"I'll bring wood for the fire," he said, and stepped outside.

The Sun was rising, and a quiet peace lay over the homes along the riverbank. The tinkle of bells filled the air as the herds of goats and sheep moved out of their corrals toward the river. The sweet smell of kitchen fires spiced the air.

Jalamanta raised his arms in thanksgiving. He asked the light of the Sun to bless all of life.

The Lords and Ladies of the Light came streaking across space to bathe everything in radiant light. They danced on the leaves of the trees, and the glow across the sage desert was a light alive with essence. All across the valley and toward the mountain the land was alive with the light.

Jalamanta thanked the Universal Spirit for the day, thanking the Sun for its reflection of light. The beauty of the morning was testament to the soul of the Earth, the soul of the universe.

He raised his axe and split the sweet red wood, and the ring of his axe joined the symphony of the new day: the birdsong in the trees, the bleating of goats, the call of the children.

He carried an armload of wood in and placed

the kindling on yesterday's embers. The fingers of fire rose.

Together they prepared their meal, and when they had finished, they let the goats out of their pen. They worked in rhythm, as if they had worked together for a long time.

"I had a dream of love," he told her, his voice soft in the sweetness of the desert morning.

"I had the same dream." She smiled.

"One must listen to one's dreams," he said. "It told me I am home."

"You have always been home," she replied.

"The soul is like a well that cannot be filled," he said. "There is always more to share."

"You are that deep well, and the people will come to drink. There is a thirst in the land. There is a hunger to take back our souls from those who wield control."

"And there is a hunger in me to return to this community of friends and neighbors," he said, and looked at her. "And to learn from you, the weaver of the magic blanket."

DEATH

The news of his meeting with Benago spread quickly, so many were gathered by the river when Jalamanta and Fatimah drove their goats to drink.

"What did the inquisitor say?" the elders asked.

"He told me I undermine the dogma of the moral authorities," Jalamanta replied. "He warned me not to speak my mind."

"Will you obey him?" they asked.

"I obey the dictates of my soul," Jalamanta answered.

The elders nodded their approval.

"Benago has grown old in his quest for power," one of the elders said. "He fears death."

"Ay, we all fear death," another said.

They turned to Jalamanta. "Is the fear of death natural?" they asked.

Jalamanta looked at them and then at a field of sunflowers that grew along the riverbank.

"Look at the plants the Sun and Earth have nourished. When their season is done, the elements return to the Earth, but the light of the flower commingles with a greater light. The animals that run free in the forest are also guided by the seasons of time. Even the highest mountain erodes to the tune of time. The passage of time moves galaxies through empty space, and the music of those spheres is time itself, and all is as it should be."

"Death is part of the natural cycle," one of the elders said, and nodded.

"Yes, even the Sun obeys a cycle that reflects the dying and the renewal. At winter solstice the Sun is at its southernmost point. It appears to die. Raise your voices in prayer on that day when the Sun stands still. Pray the Sun be made strong and return to bless our mother Earth. The death of the spirit is reflected in the death of the Sun, but contemplation of the Source of Life assists the Sun in its return. Contemplation of your soul renews it."

"So even time dies," a man said, "and the time of the Fifth Sun will come to an end. So the old prophets said. Is it true?"

The people shuddered. In the memory of their group, they had always feared the end of time. If time ended, even the greatest works of the rulers, the builders, the artists would be erased. Everything would cease to exist.

Within the arms of time, they had seen loved ones die, but the group continued; but if time died, it must mean the end of everything. Memory would die. Dreams would die. All would die.

"We have constructed civilizations and great works of art," Jalamanta said, "and we have given each age its name according to its achievements and its gods. But everything is bound to a cycle of time that brings birth, growth, and death."

"What is time?"

"The cycle of time is the passage of light, and that which abides is the spirit. What we call death is a cycle of time completing itself, a season of the soul. Do not worry over its passage. You cannot change the seasons of time. The body dies, but the soul lives on, returning to the cosmic wind and the light that sweeps around the universe."

"Is there no reward for those of us who have lived good lives?" a woman asked.

"The stories our ancestors told described a heaven," Jalamanta said, "a transcendent place that was their idea of a return to the First Creation. The mind creates its images of heaven and hell. The mind is artful and powerful, but once freed of the flesh, it dies. The soul remains. The body returns to the Earth, but the soul is gathered into the cosmic wind, a gentle breeze of souls celebrating their source, the First Light. Like the universe converging on its center, the Earth energy of spirits converges to the center."

"Can the individual soul return to Earth?" an old man asked. "Some of the old philosophies speak of reincarnation, and now that I am old, I see how much work I have yet to do. Is there another life?"

"The mind desires to live forever. The soul already knows it does," Jalamanta said. "Our light within is a reflection of the soul of the universe, and so it is part of the consciousness of the universe. Do not allow the desires of the body to trap you. Each day you are contributing to the expanding consciousness of the universe. This is your purpose. Allow peace to enter your soul today."

The old man was not satisfied. "I desire another life," he persisted. "It doesn't seem fair to know so much of this life and have so much left to do, and then have it all end. I fear death," he admitted. "I don't want to die."

Jalamanta took pity on the old man. He embraced him and touched his forehead to the forehead of the man, and the reservoir of light that he carried in his soul passed to the old man. That simple human touch filled him with new strength.

"The light of your soul is a reflection of the eternal light of the Cosmos. Guard the light as one would cup a lighted candle from the wind. Let it glow and clarify your path. But when the body dies, the light must move into the stream of light circling the universe. Your body will be like the plant that dissolves back to the Earth, but your soul will be integrated into the encompassing consciousness that converges to the All."

The film of fear disappeared from the old man's eyes. Jalamanta had pulled away a veil, exposing the soul of the old man and letting him look into the light within that does not die.

"The light within has no season, no time. And so the soul has no season, no time. It cannot die," Jalamanta said.

"Thank you," the old man replied, and for the first time in many years, he sat peacefully by the edge of the river and contemplated the beauty of nature, the brilliance of the sunlight on the water. The pain of the flesh eased, and his soul opened to gather light for the journey he no longer feared.

"Is there a ceremony when the soul departs?" a daughter asked.

"Return the ashes to the Earth," Jalamanta replied. "Go to a favorite place of that person. There, where his soul was nourished by the beauty of the Earth, you should spread the ashes."

"Should we grieve?" the daughter asked.

"Grief expresses itself in the heart," Jalamanta answered. "But do not let it become a veil that shrouds the soul of the living. The gathering of friends alleviates the grief. On the first day, the cremation is prepared. On the second day, the cremation is carried out and delivered to the place. On the third day, the ashes are scattered. During this ceremony you should sing and rejoice. In your contemplations remember the good deeds of the person. Each day you must pray in one of the sacred directions of the universe. On the fourth day, the ceremony is ended and the living return to their homes.

"When you spread the ashes, you are returning to the Earth the temple of the soul, and the Earth will receive it. Those four days the soul lingers near the love that nourished it on Earth. The soul, too, had grown accustomed to the Earth, so it is near you. Your songs will assist its departure. It must return to the cosmic wind, return to the energy of the universe. The soul should not remain haunting those who remain on Earth. It should return to the eternal light of the universe."

"Some say the soul inhabits another body when its present body dies," a woman who knew of possession by the spirit said. "That is why in this life events or places are often very familiar to us. We have been here in a prior life."

Jalamanta nodded. "The philosophers of the East have taught of the transmigration of the soul. I say, why fret that your soul will go to heaven or hell or be born again in another body. Know that you have only this immediate season of time in which to nourish your soul and seek clarity. When the soul becomes God, it joins the spiritual consciousness of the universe."

"The essence may know, but the mind protests," the doctor of philosophy reminded him.

"The mind is the conscious ego of the soul for its time on Earth, and it has great power, but it is not immortal like the soul."

"Your thoughts inspire," the doctor of philosophy said, "but I believe the mind is stronger than the soul. The mind can destroy the flesh, and the body in deep pain has been known to destroy the mind."

"The mind is part of the trinity of mind, body, and soul, but it is so powerful that it struggles for ascendancy. In this era, which glorifies the material world, mind and body have been raised to supreme heights. 'What I conceive, I can create,' says the mind to the willing flesh, and the more they create, the greater their arrogance. This age of violence and destruction of the Earth testifies to that."

"But our minds have created science, medicine, and a technology to help mankind," a scientist said. "We have alleviated much sickness and disease, fed mankind, plunged to the depths of the sea, and soared to the planets."

"I applaud the mind," Jalamanta said, "and understand its desire for knowledge and power. But you have been giving only the mind its credit and forgotten the peace of the soul. Mind, soul, and body should act as one in the enlightened person."

"I understand and improve my body," a young Adonis said, and flexed his muscles. He glowed in the sheen of youth. "But I don't know how to care for the soul."

"There is beauty in the body," Jalamanta agreed, "for the body is the temple of the soul, and you must care for it. And the mind, like the soul, must be enlightened. But when flesh and mind forget they serve the soul, the path is made difficult."

"Are you saying the soul exists before the mind?" the scientist asked.

"The soul partakes in and is fed by the light of the Universal Spirit, as the mind partakes in and is fed by the body. The soul came from the cosmic consciousness of the universe, the mind is born with the body."

"But the mind can describe the soul."

"Yes, the mind is a wonder of creation, and so powerful it can contemplate the soul. Mind can turn on the essence within and describe it. And as the flesh is the temple of the soul, so its function is of prime importance. But if the mind or the body grow too independent and forget the principal essence, then the soul is clouded by veils and weakened."

A young woman stepped forward. "I like beautiful things, and I like to please others with my beauty. Is that wrong?"

"Your beauty is a reflection of your soul. Like a crystal shining in the sun, the soul has many facets. The desirous egos are facets of the soul. When the yearnings of the egos grow too strong, the soul is cluttered and confused. It loses sight of its true goal: to follow the Path of the Sun toward perfect clarity, the higher consciousness. Exercise the mind, for the rational mind is capable of divulging much beauty. It, too, is a channel of light and energy to the soul, for it loves contemplation. And exercise the body, for it is united to the soul when the body is conceived. But do not lose sight of the soul's purpose. When one's season is done on Earth, the body returns to the Earth, and the mind's knowledge ends. The soul as essence lives on and continues its journey to the center."

PROPER
CONDUCT

The elders asked Jalamanta to speak of the conduct a good person should practice.

"Many wiser men and women before me have come to teach you proper conduct," Jalamanta replied. "Books are full of the laws of conduct and ethics. Codices on morality abound. And yet, one law serves all: Love one another. Each person reflects the other, because the souls are kindred spirits. Our era has forgotten this, and we have become confused with the desires of the material world, the shadows of illusion."

"What are these shadows?" a woman asked.

"The shadows are the surface of things. We see the colors of people, the religion they practice, their history and cultural ways, their nation or tribe, whether rich or poor. We have learned to judge other by those surfaces. I say, greet and love others, and realize you share the same light within."

"You are a desert wanderer," a man said, "You have no worldly possessions. Here on the outskirts of the city, your are with the poor and the workers. We listen to you. But in the inner circles, people are judged by their wealth. The wealthy will laugh at you."

"Yes," another man agreed. "The rich man believes he is better than the poor man. Around us tribes massacre each other to protect their territories or their religions. Even the color of one's skin is condemned. Mankind will never subscribe to this simple rule you preach. Our acquisitive nature and our desire for power will finally destroy us."

Others in the crowd nodded sadly. The world was filled with violence. Some doubted the soul and its transcendent calling. Man's worst nature ruled, and the atrocities committed on men, women, and children were testament to that. Even their own City of the Fifth Sun was under attack from a neighboring nation. Dispute ruled the world in this age of violence.

"Let's face it," another man added, "the world is ruled by might. He who is strong dictates the morality of the day."

"Man can build the weapons of war to protect himself, but the soul builds the path of peace," Jalamanta said.

"How did we come to feel so alienated from each other?" the man asked.

"The body individualizes its own energy and creates a strong will that desires its own survival," Jalamanta said. "Thus it creates aloneness. Each mind is wrapped in its own shell, and each sees itself as the only unity. This is natural to man. But the greatest power is the power of the soul, for the soul can break through this cocoon of aloneness."

"The clarity we share this morning will give us strength," a woman said. "I have felt this community of souls. I feel a peace with my neighbors I have never felt before."

"The weapons of war and bombs destroy the peace," a cynic said, and laughed.

"When you give in to that pessimism," Jalamanta said, "you cover yourself with the veils of fear and doubt. You separate yourself further from your fellow human beings. False leaders work to convince you this is the only way. You must fight back."

Was it possible? The people wondered. For a long time the state of the world had been under siege, and even the fabled City of the Sun, which had been built from the sweat and labor of so many different groups, was now dying.

"I believe that," the woman who spoke of peace said. "The peace I feel suggests possibility." She turned to Jalamanta. "Is there any hope?"

"The soul that walks on the Path of the Sun puts pessimism and cynicism behind," Jalamanta answered. "Violence, in all its aspects, exists because you allow it. Open your souls to the light of the Sun. Feel the power of love that is created by clarity. Turn and greet your neighbors as you would greet yourself. This community of souls will create the power of love you need to usher in the era of the Sixth Sun. Yes, there is hope, for as one era of time dies, a new dawn is on the horizon."

"You say we can create this new era," the woman said, and touched Jalamanta's hands.

"Yes. Our evolution is always toward a higher consciousness. For us it means a new humanity. We are creatures of the Earth and the light of the Sun. Without our struggle to do what is right, the negative forces and veils will cover the Cosmos."

"The era of the Sixth Sun," the woman pondered. "What will it be like?"

"It is what we create," Jalamanta answered. "It can be an era of peace and harmony. A time filled with the true love that emanates from the community of souls."

The crowd grew sober. They had listened to Jalamanta, and if they understood him correctly, the destiny of the world lay in their hands. Turning to greet each other as neighbors and joining in the community of the souls had wider implications.

Their actions would be like the ripple of a stone dropped in a pond; they were the stone and the Cosmos was the pond. Not only peace and unity could be brought to Earth by their good acts, but the universe could be affected. It was a struggle within each individual to tear away the veils, and as each did so, the universe was recreated.

The higher consciousness and the enlightened humanity the prophet spoke of would flow toward the Center. In the Center lay Unity, Peace, Truth, and Divine Love, which inspired the birth of the universe. The Center was reached by illuminating each soul and allowing the imaginative power of light to shine within.

Jalamanta had said the Earth and the universe have a soul, they are alive with the same energy that fills each person. It was time to turn humanity away from chaos and violence; it was time to fill the soul with clarity and to join with others. Thus would the new era of light be created.

THE
ANCESTORS

Can we not go to our temples of worship and find solace?" a woman asked.

"If there is solace in your community of believers, then join with them," Jalamanta answered. "But do not lose your soul to the dogma of those who profess to hold the only truth. The truth is all around us and is revealed to the soul on the Path of the Sun."

"Are you establishing a new church?" the woman asked.

"No," he replied, "I walk on the Path of the Sun, the Earth is my church, the Sun is a prism that reflects the Divine Love of the universe. The contemplation of the Lords and Ladies of the Light may be done in a rich man's mansion or by the poor in their abode."

"When my people came to the Seventh City of the Sun, they brought with them their pantheon of saints," a woman said. "Here they found the native people performed ceremonies for their ancestral spirits and their deities. The saintly people of the past are our guides, my mother taught me. I pray to the saints as she taught me."

"And I say your mother has become a saint," Jalamanta replied.

The woman wondered if she had heard correctly. "My mother was a kind person, and she did good all her life, but why do you call her a saint?"

"Those we call saints and prophets are good men and women who have allowed the clarity of light to fill their souls," Jalamanta said. "Your mother filled her soul with light and did good works. Her spirit is near you in time of need."

"Our parents can become saints?" the woman asked.

"The souls we have known are the souls of those closest to us. We turn to them in times of need. Their souls are now the energy of the universe, and so their light can help us in this time of violence."

"I worship my ancestors," a man said. "I feel them near me."

"The ancestors whose spirits have departed become guides in the cosmic wind that sweeps the universe. They have returned to the clarity of the First Light. In our dreams and hopes, they return as guides to fill us with light."

A whisper rippled through the crowd. Jalamanta

was extending a saintly mantle to those good people who filled their souls with light and who had treated their neighbors as themselves.

Many in the crowd had felt this. In times of trouble or deep trauma, the voices of those departed came to whisper and to guide. Those souls came to assist in times of need. The ancestors were entities whose whispers lent strength to the soul.

"Your own loved ones, wise teachers you have known, physicians who have healed the infirm, your father or mother, or friends who have walked the path of clarity. Their souls are saintly. To honor them is another way of expressing our love for those who did good on Earth," Jalamanta said.

"But all are not so friendly," another woman spoke. "I am haunted by my mother's spirit. She blamed me for her suffering on Earth. Now she is dead and will not let me go."

"She died shrouded by veils," he said, "and so even now her soul struggles for clarity. Her soul has attached herself to you. During her life on Earth, her soul was shrouded by veils of doubt. Now she seeks release. Such souls must be exorcised. They must leave their haunting and join the cosmic wind."

A man came forward. "Not all the people you name are saintly. My father abused and beat me as a child. Even now, in my nightmares, I feel his wrath. How can I forgive?"

"Forgiveness is the first step in releasing these violent souls who did not know the light while on

Earth," Jalamanta said. "Join with me and with our friends. Our circle will pray together, and this cleansing will release those souls fastened to yours."

He asked those present to gather in a circle. Holding hands, they prayed for the woman and the man to be released of the haunting souls. The people prayed for light to prevail, each one in private passed the strength of light within to the man and woman.

When the ceremony was completed, the spirits that had attached to the woman and the man were winging their way toward their natural evolution.

"I feel as if a weight has been lifted," the woman said with a smile, and she thanked the community of souls she had just joined.

And the man also thanked the group. "I feel I am alone no longer," he said.

LOVE

When the ceremony was done, a young couple stepped forward.

"We are in love, and we desire each other. But now that you have spoken of the love one soul should have for another, we worry that our love is only of the flesh. Tell us, what is love?"

"Love is the bonding of souls," Jalamanta answered. "When one soul meets another and love binds them, then the wall of separation crumbles. Two souls are in love when they dissolve one into the other. Then we realize the potential of love, for now the energy of the soul turns to its communal work. Two will become a family, and family will join the community."

"So the community of souls begins when two souls find each other," a woman said.

"Yes," Jalamanta answered.

He looked at Fatimah. During his years as a desert wanderer, he had kept her constantly in mind. She was the Holy Grail of his dreams; she guarded the love of their youth. He knew that their love was strong enough to withstand the separation of the years.

She looked at him, and her gaze told him that she, too, had kept him in her dreams. All else, time could cover. The ancient gods and kings of prior civilizations were hidden under the sands of the desert. They had already disappeared from the memory of the people. Only the binding love of souls remained as a testimony to the humanity of the people.

Holding hands, the lovers stood in front of Jalamanta. They were lovers who felt their souls belonged to each other, but they also felt the desires of the flesh. The words of Jalamanta confused them. Did he mean that only the souls should enjoy the intense desire they felt for each other?

"Speak," the young woman encouraged her beloved gently. "Tell him our thoughts."

"Our love is a burning need," the young man said, looking into the eyes of his beloved.

"When I am with him, I want to touch him and hold him close," the young woman said. "I want to consume him."

"The soul in love is full of passion," Jalamanta said. "When the veils have been stripped away and the windows of the soul opened, then the beloved is invited in. The love of one soul for the other may remain spiritual: the child's love for the parent and the parent's love for the child, the acolyte's love for the Universal Spirit, the mystic's union with the Transcendent, the student's love for the teacher, the patient's love for the doctor. In such relationships the soul's love is spiritual."

"Then it is wrong for our bodies to desire each other so much?" the young woman asked.

"No," Jalamanta said and placed his hands on the lovers' shoulders. "The desire of the flesh is as beautiful as the desire of the soul. While the soul is in the body, body and soul are one. Love is an expression of unity. The desire of one body for the other is as true a passion as we can know on this Earth. Celebrate the passion of the body, for that love is an expression of the soul's essence."

The young couple smiled and embraced each other. Jalamanta had blessed their spiritual love for one another, and the desire their bodies felt.

A murmur rippled among some in the crowd, those who had taught the flesh was evil and its ways sinful.

Iago, who had been listening carefully, stepped forward, thinking he had found another mistake in Jalamanta's teaching.

"This is wrong," he said, "you are encouraging the uncontrolled sexuality that plagues the young."

"The soul dwells within the body," Jalamanta answered. "The body is the temple of the soul, and it has its role in our worldly and spiritual evolution. The body's fulfillment is also passionate. When passion of the flesh blends with passion of the soul, a deep and binding love is experienced. Love breaks the shell of separation and leads us to our true humanity."

"But you yourself spoke against this age of materialism," Iago insisted. "Flesh is matter, the dust we become, and you assign it too high a role."

"The body *is* of the material world and will drag itself down if the passion it feels is false," Jalamanta replied. "What you are describing is the world of love shrouded by veils. When the body is viewed only as an object for sexual consummation, then the veils have clouded the soul. That love is doomed, for the souls have not opened up to each other.

"But when love draws the souls to bond, the body partakes of that union. The love of one for the other is a reflection of the Universal Spirit, the spark of love that illuminates. We are receptacles for that light, we are that very same star dust of the First Creation."

"Our love reflects the First Creation?" the young woman said. "That is a lovely vision. We are not on Earth one day and gone the next. Our love has a purpose."

"Yes." Jalamanta smiled.

He saw in the eyes of the two lovers the windows of their souls. The light of love shone for each other. He, too, knew the transcendent power of the divine in Fatimah's eyes.

The moral authorities had preached against the passion of the body, but the soul was imbedded in the body. Both soul and body felt the binding desire of love.

"Love is the creative force of the universe," Jalamanta said. "The passion of our souls and bodies reflects the First Creation. If the veils that suffocate the soul are removed, then love moves the soul on the Path of the Sun. Our path is to converge on the center, to feel the creative passion of unity. I have said that the First Creation was an imaginative act that gave birth to a universal consciousness. It was also a passionate act. So it is that in the arms of the beloved, the lover senses the essence of that unity that energizes the universe. Love renews the lover and the beloved, and with love in their hearts, both can do the work of humanity. Love makes us human, and the human touch, which is the touch of love, is the greatest miracle."

"I fear you give a license for promiscuity," Iago said, frowning. "These two are too young to know of the passion of the soul!"

"The soul reflects the light of the universe. How can it be too young," Jalamanta answered. "The young are full of the instinct of procreation, but they also feel the passion of their souls. When the veils are stripped away, the lovers will know the responsibility they bear each other. To sustain each other's soul is the work of love. This they must know. Those who have preached the subservience of women forget all souls are equal."

Many nodded. Love was the prime ingredient in the community of souls, and so the work of humanity progressed. The soul was forever, but it resided in the body, and Jalamanta ascribed passion to both. Seek unity, he said, strip the veils, and join the souls in love.

Iago shook his head. All these years he had desired Fatimah, and unable to have her, he preached against the sins of the flesh. Now Jalamanta had returned to say the flesh, too, took part in the evolution of the soul.

"Love one another," Jalamanta said to the lovers. "Love in the spirit of humanity. Love one another as mates, in the spirit of your bodies. Nothing is sinful when love opens the window of the soul. The center is described as love. What you feel for one another is love. As a lover loses his aloneness in the beloved, so he learns to lose it in the spiritual union with others. That passionate joining creates a higher consciousness; it creates the path of humanity."

Jalamanta blessed the lovers, and they thanked him. He turned to Fatimah and took her hands.

"I have loved this woman since my soul was opened to her love. What do you say of love?" he asked.

"I say what you have said to this young couple. When we were young, the veils that covered our souls were removed by our love. That attraction was instant. The merest touch told us we were to be lovers. There is communion of the souls, and there is communion of the flesh. During this time of your exile, I have felt my soul flying to be with you."

Jalamanta smiled. Her radiant smile was as beautiful as it had been thirty years ago. He kissed her hands, and now they sat for a moment in silence.

He understood that the Holy Grail he had seen in his dreams was the soul of Fatimah. Desert wanderers since time immemorial had come to the same discovery: they went in search of the chalice that held the most profound mystery of the universe, and they found that the cup of shining gold held the soul of their beloved. Thus the Universal Spirit moved in their midst.

"Love one another," Fatimah said.

In that moment of contemplation, the beauty of the morning revealed itself again. The Lords and Ladies of the Light infused the Earth with shining light. Trees, water, birdsong, the call of the sheep and the goats, the fish in the river, mountain, and stone, all shimmered in that ecstatic moment.

LOVE
OF THE
EARTH

After the Sun's epiphany, many in the crowd rose refreshed. The encumbrances of so many years of dogma and doctrine fell away as dark shrouds. The words of Jalamanta were simple and direct. The mystery of the universe and its unity moved through them, even now.

They looked around and found great beauty in the Earth. Peace and harmony and unity were possible. Around them, the Earth was being devastated by the madness of those who could not see. They did not see the Earth as the beloved of the Sun; they did not see the Earth as the Holy Grail.

The new era would have to teach that Earth and Sun and Cosmos were one. Removing the veils would allow a view into the Unity.

The people knew they had forgotten this love of

the Earth. The Earth too had a soul, Jalamanta said. The universe had a soul. All was touched with spirit.

"Speak to us of this love you have for the Earth," Fatimah said.

She, too, felt that the spirit that moved through her moved through the Earth. Daily tending her goats at the edge of the desert, she watched the rhythms of sunlight bring the seasons, and she felt connected to the soul of the mountain, the desert, the river valley. Even in the harshest of weathers and in the most difficult of times, she was a daughter of the Earth.

During her moments of contemplation, she had felt Jalamanta moving closer toward her. Time and space had not severed the bonding of their souls.

"When the Lords and Ladies of the Light shine in the morning, I am joined to the animated soul of the Earth. Those moments of contemplation become a time of ecstasy," Jalamanta said.

"You say the Earth and the Cosmos are conscious, animated by a soul," a man who studied the stars said. "Science teaches us the only knowledge we have of the creation is through mathematical rules."

"The beauty of formulas is the mystery they reveal," Jalamanta said. "But the soul cannot be explained in formulas. In the mystic moment the soul speaks to us. It relates us to Unity, and that Unity is a commingling of our souls with the Universal Light. When we join together, it is a commingling of souls."

"If I study the laws of the universe, I can arrive

at that moment when the universe came into existence," the man said.

"In your soul you already reflect that first moment," Jalamanta replied.

"My soul reflects the first moment of creation?" the man said in surprise. He was a man of science who had not heard the earlier conversations on the soul.

"Yes. The soul is the crystal that gathers the light of the Sun. It is a spark of light from the First Creation. You reflect the beauty of the mathematical formulas you love, you reflect the light and the Divine Love of the Cosmos. And you reflect the soul of the Earth and its beauty."

"This light fills the Cosmos, so can there be another Earth with life like ours?" the man asked.

"It may be that the vital energy has touched foreign planets," Jalamanta replied. "And that may someday be made known to us. Speculation, theories, and even contemplation are acts of the mind meditating on origins. But the soul reflects Earth knowledge. We recognize the mystery of the creation and stand in awe of it. And yet we have lost sight of the Earth knowledge that is rooted in the soul of the Earth."

"The Earth has a soul? As each person has a soul?" the man questioned. "How can this be?"

"The essence of the First Creation, the vital energy of love flowing throughout the universe, and the cosmic wind that constitutes the souls of our ancestors also animates the soul of the Earth. Our kind, and all of life on Earth, evolved from earthly matter. Only love can make matter come to life. Yes, the Earth has a nourishing soul. The vital energy touched the Earth and brought matter to life."

A young man wrapped in a bright blanket stood. He and his group had come each day to listen to Jalamanta. He was with a small group of natives whose ancestors had originally inhabited the land. Now their numbers had dwindled, and some of the teachings of their ancestors were lost. But they kept this faith in the Earth soul; they knew Earth knowledge in their hearts.

"You are right to speak of the Earth knowledge," he said. "Our ancestors taught us that the Earth nourishes us, and the Sun activates life. And what you call the Universal Spirit we call the Great Spirit. Your teachings are close to ours, and yet you are not of our tribe."

"All tribes are one," Jalamanta said. "This is what the elders of the southern desert teach. In the past, each tribe gave the Universal Spirit different names. Each described their God to suit their need for communion with the Transcendent. But those names and descriptions of God caused divisions and wars. I say the light that is the soul is the same in every person."

"Do you believe in our Great Spirit?" the native asked.

"Yes," Jalamanta replied. "You believe your Great Spirit has animated the universe and given us the Earth as mother, the Sun to warm us, the firmament to know the expanding beauty of the First Creation. By whatever name, the Unity that binds us is the same.

"The Earth is mother because like the womb of time that received the spark of First Creation, the Earth received the spark of love that radiates throughout the universe. The Earth nourished that spark and gave it to us as our gift. It is the gift of love the mother has for her children. We reflect the essence of the center and the essence of the Earth. Soul and flesh."

"How do we learn of this Earth knowledge?" a man asked. "Our native neighbors seem to understand it, but I would like to feel it."

"Our humanity is rooted in the Earth," Jalamanta replied. "The Lords and Ladies of the Light deliver a blessing upon the Earth. As we are filled with this radiating light, our souls blossom. The same light nourishes our bodies. We are like plants, using the energy and passing it on, binding together the poles of matter and spirit. We integrate and thus enhance our consciousness. Earth knowledge is the love we have for the Earth, the love we have for each other."

The native people nodded their approval. They surrounded Jalamanta and burned incense, the sweet grass of the river, and they sang. Their elders gave thanks to the Great Spirit. A new community with hope in its heart was forming in the villages along the river. Perhaps it was not too late to give definition to the era of the Sixth Sun.

KINDRA,
THE WITCH

That evening after they had finished supper and were enjoying the cool breeze from the river, they saw a woman coming up the path. A handsome, silver-haired dog loped closely at her side.

"It is Kindra, the healer," Fatimah said.

Kindra stopped at the entry. "Good evening. May I enter?" she asked.

"Come in," Fatimah said as they rose to greet the woman.

"Wait here," Kindra said to the dog, and he sat to wait patiently for his mistress.

"I have come to speak to the man who says he is not a prophet," she said.

Jalamanta smiled and greeted her. "The titles of the world bear heavy on us and often keep us from our work. Enter and share your thoughts with us."

He greeted her in the old way, offering a thanksgiving of friendship.

"It pleases my soul to meet another on the Path of the Sun," he said, and she repeated the greeting.

He offered her a seat, and when they were settled, Fatimah offered her a cup of the fig tea they were drinking.

Kindra took the cup and sipped.

"I have been listening to your conversations with the people," she said. "I want to share my thoughts with you, but I fear many don't understand my way."

"In the circle of the community of souls, all may speak," Jalamanta said. "What is it the people would not understand?"

Kindra looked from Jalamanta to Fatimah and said, "They say I am a witch."

"You are a healer," Fatimah said. "You have knowledge of the soul." Turning to Jalamanta she continued, "When I was told our son had disappeared, I grew despondent. Kindra counseled me. Without her help the depression would have overwhelmed me."

Jalamanta touched the woman's hands. "The care you have given my beloved, you have given me. Speak freely with us."

Kindra drew near and looked into Jalamanta's eyes.

She was a healer, a shaman, and she had helped many people. Like the prophet, she had come to the conclusion that spiritual injury to the soul was the most prevalent illness.

Injury to the body could be cured with the juices of herbs, or poultices and massage. The science of medicine could heal much of the body's injuries. But injury to the soul was caused by the soul who left the path of light. The soul could injure itself, or other souls could hurt it. Those who did not know the way of the soul could not heal the spiritual illness that plagued the world.

"In my life," Kindra began, "I have found my relationship to the animal world. I have found a way to reach the guardian spirits of the animal world. They are useful in my healing. My guardian spirits are not only the souls of my teachers and ancestors, they are also the spirits of animals from the primal world. That world is my inheritance, so why should it not be available to me. There is great power in the world of the animals, the trees, the streams, and the mountains," she intoned.

Jalamanta nodded. "There are many shamans in the southern desert who teach this affinity. I have seen men and women grow strong as they journeyed with their animal spirits to cleanse their souls of negative powers."

"Yes." Kindra smiled. "But the moral authorities castigate those who speak of kinship to the animal world. They call such notions pantheism and accuse us of devil worship. There is no devil in the animals. That ugly power hides itself in men!"

"The animals are innocent," Jalamanta said. "They are part of our inheritance on Earth. They live within the bounty of the Earth knowledge. We, too, once lived within that bounty, but we have become separated. We have built a wall between us and the other animals."

"Ay." Kindra nodded and sipped the fig tea sweetened with honey. She felt at ease now. She knew Jalamanta would listen.

"The dogmas have separated us from the world we share with animals," she said. "Instead of unity, there is now separation. Under the guise of civilization, men on Earth have created a hierarchy, and those placed at the bottom of this scale are used to serve the purposes of those who place themselves high on the scale."

"Your knowledge has led you to the world of guardian spirits as it was known by our ancestors long ago," Jalamanta said.

"Yes," Kindra replied. "As the religions of the Earth grew and spread, they adopted some of the old spiritual ways of the early tribes. But they also rejected many important things. They rejected our kinship to the animals. Hunting was no longer the taking of life of a brother or sister animal to feed the family, it became a business. Now the moral authorities say the animals are beneath us! It was the serpent that caused the Fall, they say. Imagine blaming the serpent, the bearer of Earth energy and intuition. The serpent came to enlighten us with the intuitive knowledge of the Earth, not to imprison us."

"Tell us of this kinship you have found," Jalamanta said.

"I live on the mountaintop," Kindra said, pointing to the mountain in the east. "My meditations take place in the forest. All around me I hear the animals speak. I sense their power. Our history and memory were formed in that world, but the religions that created a personal God have forgotten this. They fear the energy of the animal world, and so they denounce it.

"My world is close to nature. Like you I see the vital energy of the universe filling the Earth and imbuing it with its spirit. As you have said, rock and mountain, river and fish, animal and person, all partake in the spirit. Nature is alive with that spirit."

"But the authorities fear this pantheism will take us back to making offerings to tribal deities," Fatimah said.

"Pantheism is our inheritance," Jalamanta said. "The spirits of the many souls we see in the dance of light are that infusion of the spiritual in nature."

"It is so," Kindra said, and told her story. "When I was a child, I heard stories of people who were called witches. One of the powers of a witch was to take the form of an animal. A witch could turn into a coyote, an owl, a jaguar, or other animals of the forest. In this way the witch traveled great distances. Later, when I studied the way of the shaman, I understood that the stories were not about witches but about healers. A shaman is a healer. And the forms of the animals they took

161

were really the guardian animal spirit in the world of nature.

"Each one of us has an animal guardian spirit in nature. That guardian spirit can lend us its power when we are in need. The world of healing the soul is the world of the shaman, who is a healer. Our role is to help lost souls. The stories that ascribe evil to us were concocted by ministers who feared the powers of nature.

"The world of nature is our world, but many of the ministers of the authorities denounce it as unworthy. They have built a pyramid from Earth to heaven. At the top they place their personal God. At the bottom the animals."

Jalamanta nodded. He had heard the stories from the old people of the desert tribes. In all their stories they told of their close tie to nature, and for them nature was the entire realm of Earth and sky. The guardian spirits of the animal world were also reflections of the soul of the Earth, a potent force that could help in time of need.

He was pleased to hear the woman speak. The age of science had long ago renounced the spirit within, and many of the religions no longer believed in the old ways of healing.

"You have shared part of our Earth inheritance with us," Jalamanta said to the woman.

"And you have come to bring us together," Kindra said. "I came to thank you for your message."

"We create so many divisions in our life," he said with a nod. "I came to speak of the soul because we live in an age of the fragmented soul. Violence harms the body and fragments the soul. There are many doctors who help heal a broken body, but few who have the knowledge to deal with the wounded soul. You have found this power of the guardian spirits to help people."

"The guardian spirit is that part of the soul that can go in search of the lost soul," Kindra said. "One returns to the underworld with the strength of the animal spirit as a guide. The purpose is always the same, to recover the lost or haunted soul. To create the unity you speak of."

"She has helped many people," Fatimah said, "and still the authorities don't let her rest. Only in the mountain is she safe."

"There are many ways to heal the injured soul," Jalmanta said. "Whatever sheds light on the soul is good, for once the light shines within, the soul begins its own healing. You help the fragmented soul recreate its center. The soul is so deep and profound that we only now begin to sense its vastness. It has been shaped by the Earth knowledge, and so it reflects the primal world."

"Thank you," Kindra said, and rose to leave. "I came to speak my thoughts and you have listened. There are others like me who search for ways to understand our spirits and our connection to the Earth. So many souls, as you say, are fragmented. Torn apart by violence. More and more people

RUDOLFO ANAYA

turn to simpler ways of healing, and those healing ways are in the old tradition."

She stepped close to Jalamanta and asked his blessing, and he touched his forehead to hers. The kiss of life, a kiss of sharing in the force of life.

Then she embraced Fatimah, and they, too, touched foreheads.

"I go full of a new energy," she said, smiling, and stepped into the dark. She called her dog. The sleek animal whose coat shone with moonlight followed her down the path.

THE
FRAGMENTED
SOUL

The news spread that Jalamanta came every morning to the river to offer his prayers to the Sun and that he spoke of the care of the soul. Those thirsting for answers in the age of violence flocked to the meeting place.

Now large crowds awaited Jalamanta and Fatimah as they drove their goats to the river. People came from the city itself, risking the scrutiny of the moral authorities, and possible punishment. The old natives of the land, who had withdrawn deeper into the often inhospitable hills, sent their medicine men to the gathering. Representatives from the tribes along the river began to appear.

The next morning a large crowd had gathered. Fatimah pointed to the representatives of the moral authorities who stood at the edge. They were conspicuous in their brown uniforms, their black caps, and polished boots.

"They will report your every word," she cautioned.

"Ay, Benago's guards," Jalamanta nodded in reply. "When those in power need spies and soldiers to do their work, they show their fear and ignorance."

The elders greeted Jalamanta and Fatimah, and after a prayer of thanksgiving to the Sun, they sat and urged Jalamanta to speak further on the soul.

"We have heard you speak of the fragmented soul," a woman said. She felt her soul torn in a thousand pieces, she told Jalamanta. The brutality of the time and the murdering of children had caused her depression to deepen.

"How can we find the Center when mankind seems mad with fury and bloodletting?" she asked.

Jalamanta felt great empathy with the woman. Around them, the worst of human nature had erupted. Even the innocent were affected. The fragile soul lay exposed, fragmented by the demented urge of violence.

"If a crystal falls, it breaks into many pieces. The wounded soul is like a fragmented crystal. The light is scattered. For the soul to function, it must have a center, it must feel unity, and so the pieces must be recovered. Its wholeness must be restored."

"How?" the woman asked.

"This is the work of the healer," Jalamanta answered. "Those who know how to go in search of the fragmented soul are healers. We pay much attention to the depression that affects the mind, and there are many doctors who treat the traumas of the body. But there are few who treat the soul. Shock also affects the sensitive soul. A loved one dies, there is a tragic accident, there is the betrayal of a lover or parent, or the carnage of war creates nightmares. Fright enters the soul, and it loses the strength of its Center. The fragmented soul weakens the mind and the body."

"I understand that'" the woman said. "My husband died and I felt a great loss. I do my daily work, I eat, I sleep, but deep inside I feel torn apart from my Center. What can I do?"

"You must restore your injured soul. A healer will offer prayers to the Universal Spirit, burn sweet incense, perhaps cleanse away the fright with eagle feathers. But most important, the healer becomes a guide, someone who knows that injury to the soul means the soul has taken flight. The healer teaches you to fly to recover your soul."

The crowd listened attentively. Could this be? Yes, the old stories told of the flight of the soul. The prophet's or saint's flight to join the ecstatic union with God was the flight of the mystic soul. Lovers felt their souls take flight. In the old stories witches took the shape of birds, animals, or fireballs and flew. But these stories were ridiculed by the central authorities.

"When the soul is injured and fragmented, its Center remains," Jalamanta said. "The soul may be wounded, but it cannot be destroyed. There are many ceremonies to prepare the Center of the soul to reintegrate itself. Prayer, liturgy, meditation, the sweat lodges of the people, and more elaborate ceremonies and rituals. All serve the same purpose, to enter the dark underworld in search of the wounded elements of the soul.

"Some healers use massage, some read cards, others pray to their deities and use incense. Some use the guardian spirits in the animal world, and that spirit gives you the strength to enter the underworld to recover the fragmented pieces. The lost soul is found and brought back to the Center. Unity and harmony are restored."

"Our age causes this fragmentation of the soul," the woman said.

"Yes, our time of transition is known by the injuries it causes the soul. As we injure the mind or the body, so we injure the soul. Everywhere violence attacks the soul. The worst aggression is when we no longer treat each other as brothers and sisters. Then fright and despair enter and cause the fragmentation. Our personal souls are injured, and the communal soul is also fragmented."

"How does a person learn that the soul can fly in search of its fragmented pieces?" a man asked.

"The healer is the guide," Jalamanta answered. "With a good guide one can enter the underworld and recover the fragmented soul."

"As Christ entered the underworld after his death?" a young person said thoughtfully. "Three days in search of his soul."

"All the prophets of the past have entered the underworld in search of their souls," Jalamanta replied. "To be a prophet means one has searched for the meaning of life, and in that search one enters the dark night of the soul. One must be very strong and have a good guide to return from the underworld. But all who return have reintegated their souls, and so they are on the path of clarity. They walk on the Path of the Sun."

"Have you been to the underworld?" the same young man asked.

"Yes," Jalamanta answered. "The desert was my underworld. Each person describes that place of shadows in a different way. Everyone who has felt the fragmentation of the soul has walked in that subterranean world."

"Is the underworld hell?" a young woman asked. "A place we go to suffer? A place of damnation?"

In her nightmares she saw images of the hell described by the old books.

"The underworld is within," Jalamanta answered.

"I don't understand," the young woman said, and drew forward.

"The underworld is a place created by the mind, full of demons that are our own creations." He turned to Fatimah. "My exile injured my soul.

169

I was separated from those I loved. I was exiled to aloneness. There I doubted myself and created my crisis of faith. The animals of the night that stalked my mind were the demons of doubt and despair I had created. Your love was the guide that came to piece my soul together."

"Our souls have been in communion all these years," Fatimah said.

"How can one soul guide the other?" the woman asked.

"When your husband died, his loss entered your soul," Jalamanta said to the woman. "Grief has injured you. But you still have within yourself the power to reintegrate your soul, to recreate the unity it once felt. A guide is a person who helps dispel the injury, one who helps you journey to the center. When the pieces of the soul are collected, unity and peace are restored."

The people nodded. The soul was a powerful essence; it had the capacity of becoming God. And yet the soul was also fragile, and the wounds to it were daily. In this time of violence, many people wandered the Earth with their spirits wounded.

Fatimah and other women gathered around the woman who had lost her husband, and their presence brought relief. She understood the community of souls had a great power to fight the aloneness she felt.

"Loss is natural," Jalamanta said to the woman. "The body dies, but the soul is liberated. Find your strength within."

The woman nodded and felt the center of her soul opening to gather in the pieces of her fragmented soul. Tears came to her eyes, and she was able to reach out and thank the women for their presence and Jalamanta for his words.

"Tell us more of this flight of the soul," a scholar said. "How am I supposed to believe that the soul can take flight?"

FLIGHT
OF THE
SOUL

In memory and dream the soul takes flight," Jalamanta said. "When we are near death, the soul prepares to fly. Many who have a near-death experience describe the luminous soul flying upward to join the cosmic wind that sweeps across the universe. If the soul is not yet ready to fly, the voices in the wind return it to the body."

"What are those voices?"

"They are the voices of other souls, the voices of our ancestors."

The people wondered at his words. They all knew of one person or other who had been near death, then returned.

Jalamanta was saying there was a purpose to life. The soul itself described its purpose, and yet that conscious power in the universe and in the

Earth was so connected to the soul that it played a role in the soul's destiny.

"I understand those flights you describe in a different way," the scholar said. "By flight you describe a thought of the mind, a dream of the subconscious. Surely the soul cannot take flight."

"The mind reflects the soul. There is unity in mind, body, and soul," Jalamanta replied. "In many ways, the three are one, but it is the soul that is the center. It is the soul that reflects the light of the First Creation. When the soul is contemplative, it is the soul that flies. For this the mind must be at rest."

The scholar was puzzled and not inclined to agree. Nevertheless, he asked, "How else may the soul take flight?"

"Persons who have journeyed into the underworld in search of their souls go there with the help of a guide. The healer prepares the soul to take flight. Other guardian spirits may be called upon to assist. They can be our guides in our journey into the underworld. But the journey requires the practice of a wise shaman. Flight of the soul can be dangerous to the inexperienced."

"Must there always be a guide?" the scholar asked.

"Yes. Until the person understands his own powers."

"One can prepare one's soul for flight?" the man asked.

Jalamanta smiled. "It is not as difficult as you

imagine. Think a moment of a special place where you have been, perhaps a mountaintop, a spring, the river, or in the desert itself. These places of power are sacred. Contemplating at such a shrine, the soul may soar. Awe-inspiring beauty uplifts the soul, and the joyful soul flies. Meditation also frees the soul from its veils, just as the arrival of the Lords and Ladies of the Light creates in the contemplative soul this feeling of flight. To be filled with light is the flight of the soul."

"So the flight of the soul is not only for the masters of contemplation or those who visit a shaman?"

"That is true," Jalamanta said. "The most simple meditations are also the flight of the soul. The soul soars into light as often as it journeys to the underworld. Once free of the veils of doubt and despair, the daily meditation is to fly into the light of clarity. As light fills the soul, it understands that the filaments of morning light are the same as the light of the First Creation."

A serene peace came over the crowd. Each soul could take flight into the light. This was the trust in Self Jalamanta spoke of. Each soul could find its center.

Two lovers came forward. "We feel that sense of flight when we are together," they said. "We find the center in our love."

Jalamanta nodded. For thirty years he had been deprived of his beloved's touch, and yet the memory of Fatimah's love had been with him. In the mystic caves of the desert, when he thought the love had vanished, it returned to him. He heard her voice calling his name, their pledge of love. He came to understand that he was bonded to the woman, her soul was with him, and so he accepted the vision.

Some of the mystics of the southern desert rejected the world and all it implied. Jalamanta embraced the world, and so he kept the love of Fatimah in his heart.

"Yes," he said, "love is the bonding of two souls, and the passionate souls reflect the passion of the First Creation. Likewise, the passion of the flesh must not be denied, but understand: love is not only of the flesh, but of the soul. When both dissolve one into the other, the lovers feel the flight of the soul."

"Then there are many experiences that cause the flight," the scholar said.

Jalamanta nodded. "Moments of wisdom when we sense a true insight into the nature of things, moments of beauty, goodness, moments of truth, the act of creativity—in all these illuminations we sense the flight of the soul."

He turned to the crowd.

"Each one of you has experienced such moments. The soul is an energy that yearns for union with the community of souls. This yearning is its passion, its love. It yearns for union with the All Encompassing. The transcendent moments are the flight of the soul."

"Those are moments of deep beauty," a

woman said. "But they aren't lasting. They are only fleeting glimpses into the Transcendent Other, a brief union with the Transcendent of the universe."

"Those moments of illumination can be cultivated," Jalamanta answered. "They need not be fleeting. Those whose souls are clouded with veils are slaves of the body. They have created division, and the body folds back to the Earth. But the person who walks on the Path of the Sun and daily seeks the clarity that binds the soul to the Light will find that the soul's flight can be summoned in an instant. The more you fill yourself with light, the more the soul soars. That is true joy."

"It is the joy we need in our lives," a man said, "and for our children. We are tired of war. We are tired of the material world, which, instead of liberating us, keeps us tied like slaves to its needs!"

The people nodded. "Joy," they whispered. How long had it been since each had felt the joy of the soaring soul? How long since they had felt the liberating clarity of the community of souls?

"Does everyone have this power?" a woman asked.

"Yes," Jalamanta replied. "The thoughts I share with you are not the esoteric secrets of a jealous priesthood. I only remind you of what you know. As a child I stood by this river and was filled with the beauty of life, the mystery of its magnificence. During those moments of awe and contemplation, my soul became part of that beauty. As a young man I loved a young woman so deeply, my soul dissolved into hers, and in that union we found joy. Now I pray to the Sun each morning, and the joy of the Lords and Ladies of the Light fills my soul. Each of us has these experiences to build on. The soul yearns to fly, and that flight will take us to our goal: the joy that comes from an evolving consciousness, the joy of union with the Center."

THE DARK
NIGHT
OF THE
SOUL

But we have become a materialistic world full of violence and war," a mother said. "Matter suffocates the soul, drags it into darkness. Many people say that God died long ago. If God is dead, then is there only a dark night for the soul?"

"The death of God is imagined only if you still cling to the notion of a God who acts as man," Jalamanta answered. "The energy of the universe that flows through me is a universal soul. It cannot die."

"Then you have never doubted and been filled with anguish?" the woman said.

Jalamanta remembered the dark night of the soul he had suffered. It was the destiny of every person to come to those doubts and crises.

"I was saved from that dark night by a healer

who taught me to gather the pieces of my fragmented soul. But even as I recovered, I still felt
separated from others, and so I chose to live in a
cave in the hills. I felt I was not yet fit for human
company. Each day I rose and prayed to the Sun,
but my soul would not shine forth. Doubts of the
faith I sought still haunted me.

"The youngest daughter of the healer was
assigned to bring me a loaf of bread and a jar of
goat's milk from the monastery. Once a week she
made the trip up the steep mountain to bring my
sustenance. She was the only communication I
had with humans for a year. One day she said that
it was time for me to leave the cave in the hills and
return to people.

"At first I was puzzled. How would she know
when it was time for me to enter the world
again. I asked her, and she replied, 'It is time for
you to return to the community of souls. No one
can live alone,' and she led me down to the village."

"A child shall lead them," Fatimah whispered.

"Yes," Jalamanta agreed. "How simple the
truth."

The child had led him out of the dark cave into
the Path of the Sun. Together they had come
down from the mountain to join her family.

The people of the monastery greeted him.
They touched their foreheads to his and wel-
comed him. There his real recovery began.

"Do not blame matter for the dark night of the

soul," Jalamanta said. "Do not blame the mind, which strives to know so much. The soul that walks on the Path of the Sun expresses itself in action, and that expression is its free will. The expansion of consciousness is a will to grow into power. A weak soul will allow matter to drag it into darkness. A spirited soul will fill itself with light. That fulfillment is growth. An active soul will resist the veils that create darkness. When we do not actively walk on the Path of the Sun and seek illumination, the shadows grow stronger. Those veils can suffocate the soul and create the sickness we call the dark night of the soul. That which is not brought into the light is harmful to the soul."

"But so many of us suffer from the malaise," a man said. "Our youth finds little to live for. We see much despair."

"The assault on the soul is constant," Jalamanta said. "It stems from our aloneness. When I was alone, I suffered. When a child took my hand, I walked into the light. It is union that creates love. The soul that does not learn the union of love will strike out against others. The mind may strike out against the soul, pulling the veils around the self. Strip away the veils by turning the energy into activity! Fill the soul with light, and it will reach out for union. That reaching out is an expression of the will to be. It is an expression of the will to join with humanity."

The crowd smiled. All morning Jalamanta's words had been like sunlight, illuminating what they knew in their hearts. All that was divisive hurt the soul; to open the soul to light and to others was the way. The smiles on their faces reflected the enlightenment. The era of a new time could be created.

"What you say is that the soul eventually must cure itself," the scholar said.

Jalamanta nodded. "There are healers who understand the essence of the soul. They help by assisting the person to look into the essence. How did the injury occur? Where? Return there and recover the injured parts of the soul. But the healer is only an assistant, a guide for the time being. The Path of the Sun is open to all. I do not teach dependence. The soul reintegrates itself by actively committing itself to clarity."

"My soul has entered the dark night," a young man said. "I suffer from an incurable disease. How can the clarity of the Path of the Sun help me?"

Jalamanta reached out and touched the young man. "The sick and tired body gives in to aloneness. It may drag one deeper into the mind's inner sanctum, where veils are drawn over veils until the light is dim. The Path of the Sun brings harmony through illumination. That harmony and peace will help your soul weather the storms of your illness. But the path is not easy or instant. To reconstitute faith, one must allow clarity to enter, and one must persevere in the path."

"You give hope," the young man said. "Your touch is healing. You, yourself, are a healer."

"If I help in the healing, it is because I open my soul to yours," Jalamanta said. "The healer is the guide who teaches the soul the symbols of the underworld. There the soul gathers its injured pieces, and putting them together, it begins to gather the strength it needs for reintegration.

"The simple touch of one human to another is a sign of love. It is a powerful medicine. It is the sign of union, the assurance that aloneness need not overcome us. Greet each other with this simple touch. The touch of human kindness heals. To touch is to dissolve the aloneness. To touch is to love. It is the beginning of union."

WISDOM

The words you have spoken are full of wisdom," the scholar said. "Perhaps even I have learned something today."

"The soul yearns for wisdom, for the mind's knowledge points the way," Jalamanta said. "Our minds have thought of everything that can be expressed at this time, and yet just beyond our ken is the wisdom of the soul. The soul is creative in its active aspect. It reveals itself in its creations. Truth, beauty, goodness, and all the virtues that enoble the person are the art of the soul. And so an active soul is constantly creating a reflection of itself. What it creates is the aesthetic of the soul."

"Good men and women have sought wisdom before, but few have truly found it," the scholar agreed. "I find bits of wisdom in my books, and they bring much enjoyment. But this light you speak of may be all we need to know of true wisdom."

"It is the inner wisdom," Jalamanta said. "What you find in books is knowledge, and the mind thrives on the knowledge it accumulates. But to feed the soul you have to open it to clarity. And as we share our enlightenment, we expand its power. Just as when we share love, we expand our humanity."

"Perhaps we thought our time was already dead," the scholar said, "and yet you say that it is not too late. We may yet save it."

"Yes," Jalamanta answered, "we reflect the light of the universe. If we allow veils to keep out the light, we participate in the destruction of our humanity. But if we open our souls to light and the wisdom within, we can create the new era of time. The soul's activity is creative. It moves like a compass toward beauty and goodness. It yearns for true wisdom, for true wisdom was embodied in the First Creation."

"And each new thought is a facet to be explored," the scholar said.

"Such is the wonder of the soul," Jalamanta replied.

PARTING

The morning wore on, and still the crowd would not let Jalamanta go. The Sun climbed toward its zenith, and so the people clung to the hope in his words.

Each question explored a new facet of the crystal of understanding. The soul, that essence of life within, became clearer, and for those who had denied it for so long, the acceptance was illuminating. He had answered many questions, and still there were more to ask.

Around them they felt the community of souls take hold and develop. Their jealousies and petty quarrels fell away. They understood the energy of love could be activated for good deeds. The Seventh City of the Fifth Sun was not yet dead; the world was not yet dead. Aloneness could be conquered. The soul did not exist as lonely ego or psyche; it was deeper, older in time, a thriving of the Universal Spirit in the flesh, and it could join in the communion of salvation.

Even now as the Sun showered its light over them, they felt the light of the universe reflected in the banquet the Lords and Ladies of the Light prepared. Pure light was Divine Love.

"Stay," they whispered.

"We must rest," Fatimah said, rising and turning to Santos. She had seen the representatives of the moral authority disappear. It was not a good sign.

"Yes, yes," Santos agreed. He was concerned for Jalamanta's safety. Even now a squad of guards appeared along the main road.

Jalamanta, too, had noticed the representatives' departure. In his heart he knew the authorities would not allow him to remain. The words of the desert wanderers were always a threat to the established dogma. The powerful rulers would not stand for those who spoke of liberation of the spirit.

"Yes, it is time to tend to the business of the day," Jalamanta said. A sadness filled his heart. He had hoped too much, hoped that his exile was done. Now he knew better. He turned to Fatimah.

"Perhaps it is destined that I must leave," he said.

"Leave?" she replied in surprise. He could not leave, but in her heart she knew the dangers that awaited if he stayed.

Jalamanta turned to Clepo, the boat man. The

crippled old man had been listening attentively. Beside him sat his dog, dozing in the sun.

"Will you be ready to ferry me across the river when the sun sets?" Jalamanta asked.

"Yes, master, I am ready," Clepo answered.

"You cannot leave us," a startled Santos echoed. He looked helplessly from Fatimah to the crowd.

"No, you cannot leave us!" the elders exclaimed.

"In the desert I went from one village to another, and the people of the desert kept me safe. The keepers of the dogma had no power in those far and distant villages. Am I safe here?" he asked.

He looked from Santos to Iago and to the other neighbors gathered in the crowd.

"Yes, you are safe with us," Fatimah spoke for them, and reached out to touch him. "This is your home."

"Fatimah is right," Santos said, and jumped forward. "We will not let you go."

"It is true," one of the elders said. "You must stay and speak with us again. If danger comes, we will hide you in the catacombs we've dug in the hill."

"I will stay," Jalamanta said, and took Fatimah's hands in his. In her eyes he saw doubt. Could the elders really protect him from Benago's guards?

"We thank the man who has stripped away the veils," a woman said, moving up to touch Jalamanta.

He turned and touched his forehead to hers,

and others in the crowd also came forward to share in this kiss of friendship. Then the people dispersed, returning to work, renewed with joy, all walking with a lighter step.

"Your return has been good for us," Santos said as he watched his friends and neighbors leave. "For too long we have stumbled in the dark, losing hope. We cannot bear to think of you leaving."

He looked at Fatimah. "Perhaps you can persuade him he is safe with us. As for us"—and here he looked at Iago—"we will sit as guards each night. If Benago tries anything, we will give plenty of warning."

"Yes, yes," Iago agreed, "I will guard the first part of the night tonight. You are safe with us, Jalamanta."

"No, let Santos stand guard," Fatimah said.

Jalamanta turned and placed his hand on Iago's shoulder. "Do you have any doubts, Iago?"

"Even a man on the Path of the Sun has his doubts," Iago replied.

"Well spoken, and so I choose you to guard the first part."

"Do you have doubts?" Iago asked.

"When I look into Fatimah's eyes all my doubts disappear," Jalamanta replied, and smiling, he took her hand.

Together they walked up the hill, following the small herd of goats. They would work all day in the hills, he gathering firewood to take back home, she gathering herbs.

"He is truly a man of the Earth and of the spirit," Santos said as he watched them walk away.

"Too earthy, I think," Iago said jealously. "How can he speak of the soul and then find it in the woman's eyes?"

"I think you have not listened closely to his words." Santos laughed, slapping his friend on the back. "The soul animates the body, and both in passion create love. Their love can work miracles."

"Bah," Iago spat, and lumbered away.

BETRAYAL

When the day was done and the brilliant Sun illuminated the clouds of sunset, Jalamanta and Fatimah held hands and said a prayer of thanksgiving.

That evening as they prepared their supper, the joy of their love filled the small hut. Jalamanta would stay; his thoughts of leaving had been a doubt. He knew the authorities watched his every move, recorded his every word, but so be it.

That had been the case since he first spoke out as a young man. The true liberation did not come from teaching others of the freedom of the soul, it came from being truly free within one's self.

Now he had no fear. The last of the veils of the desert had been removed. He would live with Fatimah, sharing the love they had always shared, and he would speak to the people about creating the new era of peace.

"You are happy," Fatimah said as they sat and drank tea after their meal.

"Peace in the soul radiates happiness," he said with a smile. "Yes, I am content. I am a fortunate man. I feel safe in the circle of your love."

"But you had doubts," she said.

"As did you," he replied.

"Only because I fear for you. But if Benago should try something, Iago will warn us. The elders will hide you in the catacombs they've dug in the hills. But the authorities won't act against you. It would mean an uprising——"

Just then they were interrupted by a voice in the dark. A figure came running up the dark path.

"Fatimah, Jalamanta!" the shadow called.

They rose to greet an out-of-breath Santos, who came stumbling to them.

"Where is he?" Santos cried.

"Who?"

"Iago?"

"Sitting there at the foot of the path——"

"No. He is gone. He has betrayed you!" Santos clutched at Jalamanta.

"Iago?"

"You must flee!" Santos pulled at his friend.

"Why? What has happened?" Jalamanta asked.

"You have been accused of heresy!" Santos exclaimed. "The authorities have denounced your teachings and issued a warrant for your arrest!"

"What can we do?" Fatimah asked.

Her worst fear was realized. Even as she had tried to dispel her doubts, she had heard a voice within warning her that danger lurked nearby: Iago had betrayed him.

"He must escape!" Santos replied. "Clepo is waiting! If you can cross the river tonight, you have a chance! Come! There is no time to waste!"

He pulled at Jalamanta.

"I'll go with you," Fatimah said, gathering her shawl around her.

"No. It's too dangerous! Perhaps I was foolish to dream that I could remain here—"

"Our foolishness was to part the first time. I will go," she said, and looked into his eyes. "If you want me at your side, that's where I belong."

"I want you with me," he replied. He held her and looked into her eyes. "Is that where you want to be, at the side of a desert wanderer?"

"Yes," she replied.

"Gather what you must take."

"Hurry," Santos pleaded, "there's little time!"

"My crystal necklace and your blanket for warmth," Fatimah said, touching the necklace around her neck and gathering up the blanket. "That's all we need."

He took her arm and they followed Santos down the path toward the river. They had nearly reached Clepo's boat when a ring of lanterns surrounded them and a rough voice called for them to stop.

"Halt! We are looking for the man they call

Jalamanta!" the leader of the uniformed men shouted, and he held his lantern in Jalamanta's face. "Are you Amado, the man who calls himself Jalamanta?"

"That's him," they heard the hiss from the shadows.

Jalamanta turned and recognized Iago in the dancing light of the lanterns as two of the guards took hold of him.

"No!" Fatimah protested, but a guard held her back.

Santos leaped forward to defend Jalamanta, but one of the guards struck him with a baton and he fell to the ground.

"Do not interfere with the police," the captain in charge shouted. He turned to Jalamanta.

"Jalamanta, I arrest you by order of the authorities who are the guardians of law and order in the Seventh City of the Sun. You have preached false doctrines, telling the populace that the soul can become God. You have told them they can gather and create a community, and such a community can rule itself. Such preachings are blasphemous and seditious. I am instructed by the central authorities to bring you before the council for trial! Take him away," he commanded, nodding at the guards.

"Wait!" Jalamanta said, and the command in his voice made the guards stand back. He leaned and helped Santos to his feet. "Do not struggle, old friend. For now, it is useless. Take care of Fatimah."

Santos reached out and touched his forehead to Jalamanta's. Tears filled his eyes. "I am sorry," he whispered. "I should have stood guard."

"You are not to blame, dear friend. Betrayal is a symptom of the time," Jalamanta said. "Those with false desires in their hearts betray themselves."

"Come!" the police said, closing in again and pulling roughly at Jalamanta. Fatimah's blanket fell to the ground.

"Wait!" Fatimah cried. She stooped to pick up the blanket and placed it over Jalamanta's shoulders.

"I will be with you," she whispered, and kissed him. "Wherever you are, I'll be there."

"And I will be with you," he replied, clasping her hands in his, touching his forehead to hers.

Then the guards pulled him away, and Fatimah and Santos stood watching helplessly as the light of the lanterns and the dark figures disappeared up the road that led to the citadel.